Slocum grabbed the shaking bartender's wrist before he could pull away.

"Mind tellin' me why everybody in this town's so nervous?" he asked. He and Amos had been keeping an eye peeled for any sign of the Carthage boys, and there wasn't any. Unless they'd sent someone to warn the town they were about to invade—which was highly unlikely—this didn't make sense.

"E-everybody n-nervous?" stuttered the barkeep. "D-don't know why you'd s-say that, m-mister."

Slocum let go of his wrist, and the man practically leapt to the far end of the bar, knocking over a tray of glasses. They clattered to the floor, and the other startled customers jumped, one clean out of his chair.

"Slocum?" Amos said softly, and Slocum turned to see a new fellow entering the saloon. He was of medium height, dark-haired, and exceedingly nervous-looking—and he was wearing a deputy's badge on his vest.

"Finally," Slocum said, and turned toward him. "What the hell's going on around here, any—"

Something hit him, slamming into the back of his head, and the whole world went black . . .

JAKE LOGAN

SLOCUM
IN THE SECRET SERVICE

JOVE BOOKS, NEW YORK

This is a work of fiction. Names, characters, places, and incidents either
are the product of the author's imagination or are used fictitiously,
and any resemblance to actual persons living or dead, business
establishments, events, or locales is entirely coincidental.

SLOCUM IN THE SECRET SERVICE

A Jove Book / published by arrangement with
the author

PRINTING HISTORY
Jove edition / September 2004

ISBN: 0-515-13811-8

A JOVE BOOK®
Jove Books are published by The Berkley Publishing Group,
a division of Penguin Group (USA) Inc.,
375 Hudson Street, New York, New York 10014.
JOVE and the "J" design
are trademarks belonging to Penguin Group (USA) Inc.

PRINTED IN THE UNITED STATES OF AMERICA

10 9 8 7 6 5 4 3 2 1

1

"How'd you get a name like Tipsy, anyhow?" Slocum asked, once he'd relit his cigar.

The girl, brunette and petite, on whose bare belly the red glass ashtray balanced, giggled softly. She caught the ashtray with one hand when it threatened to bounce and slide off her belly.

"I dunno, honey," she drawled with a grin, her eyelashes batting to beat the band. "Guess my daddy had what you call one of them whimsical streaks."

"Well, Tipsy, he had one beautiful daughter, that's for sure," Slocum said. He curled his arm around her and took a fresh puff on the cigar. He figured that if he kept relighting this thing every time they stopped humping, then let it go out each time they dove back in again, it'd probably last him a week. Which was fine by him.

She giggled again. It wasn't one of those silly, girlish giggles. It was low and breathy and incredibly sexy. More of a purring rumble than a regular giggle, he thought.

"You'd best cut that out, Tipsy," he said, grinning. "You'll get me goin' again."

"Don't you want to?" she asked, and stuck out her lower lip just a tad. That pout of hers made him crazy, too.

So he looked up at the ceiling of her bright red bedroom, gave her shoulders a little hug, and said, "Sure, honey. Just like to get my bearings every once in a while, that's all."

"It's been a long time since you been through," he heard her say. "Nigh on a whole year. I missed you, Slocum."

"Me, too, Tipsy."

"So what you been doin'?" she asked. "Where do you go from here?"

"Well, been doin' a job up in Colorado," he said dreamily.

Tipsy was plumb wearing him out, that's what she was doing. He felt like a nap was in order, but he tried to stay awake and keep his eyelids from fluttering. It was only polite, after all.

He continued, "Well, I rounded up some, er, 'borrowed' cows for a man named Finster, did a little bounty work while I was at it, and right now I'm at loose ends."

He watched his smoke curl lazily upward. That was about how he felt right at the moment, like he could just float up and hover around the ceiling for a good, long while.

"And you came through Armpit just to see me?" she asked hopefully.

"Yup, Tipsy," he said, and it was the truth, too. "Ain't been thinkin' about nothin' but you, brown eyes, for the longest while."

Well, she'd been on his mind for the last couple of weeks, anyway, and he'd ridden down into Arizona and into the backwater town of Armpit—doubtless, christened by some joker—with no other purpose than to come calling on his dark-eyed Tipsy.

Smiling, she hugged him tight and they lapsed into silence, which was exactly what Slocum didn't need.

His cigar went out, and he thought he mumbled something to Tipsy about a nap. That was the last thing he remembered, at least. And then, suddenly, it was dusk and somebody had dropped a piano downstairs—or near to it, anyhow—and he was sitting bolt upright, gun in hand.

He scrambled into his britches, threw on a shirt and strapped on his gunbelt, all on the way to the door. Tipsy was nowhere in sight.

Shouts and hollers roared up the stairs, and he ran barefoot and open-shirted through a wall of growing noise, down the steps to the first floor. Immediately he ducked to avoid a flying beer mug, miraculously still half-full of beer.

It crashed into the wall directly behind him, showering him with beer and broken glass. He didn't stay put long enough to get too wet, though, because somebody bumped into him, shoving him out of the way. With a thump, he landed on his ass on the third stair.

Which was just in time to have his chest and shoulder trampled by two other customers, running down the stairs to join in the brawl.

"All right, all right!" he grunted as he worked his way back up the stairs.

Whoever's fight this was, it wasn't his. And it'd sure be a shame to get himself all bruised up and sore just when he had a nice couple of days planned with the voluptuous Tipsy Magee.

From the relative safety of the landing—safe, other than the occasional whiskey bottle or shot glass, or once, a lady's shoe, that flew in his direction—he looked over the rowdy, roiling scene below.

His first guess had been right. Somebody *had* dropped a piano. Knocked it over, anyhow. At the moment, it was mostly hidden by the bodies scrambling over it. The piano player had retreated back behind the bar. A couple of times, Slocum caught a glimpse of his green-visored head peeking up over the bar top.

Apparently everyone but him was down there having a good time. Men and gals slugged it out with no discretion and no apologies—and no compunctions whatsoever. Two fellows were stationed by the batwing doors, slinging unconscious brawlers out into the street. He looked for Tipsy, but didn't see her, couldn't even catch a glimpse of that pink dress she'd been wearing.

Before he took it off of her, he reminded himself, and smirked.

Congratulating himself on his uncommon but very wise decision to stay the hell out of this free-for-all, he fished in his pocket for his fixings pouch. He'd forgotten to bring his cigar, but if he went back to get it, he might miss something.

A storekeeper-type was tossed up into the air, limbs flailing, as Slocum licked his quirlie. The man landed atop a beer-drenched saloon gal in a red dress, its sequins dripping and its feathers a-droop. She let out a holler and pushed him off just as Slocum tried to light his lucifer on the sole of his boot—and then remembered that he was barefoot.

Belatedly, he flicked it on the green-painted wall and lit his smoke. And halfway through the quirlie, Slocum managed to catch one of those whiskey bottles that was flung in his direction, and it actually still had some contents!

Two more cowboys went flying out the door, and three fresh ones came in and joined the brawl.

"It's a grand life, ain't it?" he asked nobody in particular as he held the whiskey bottle to his lips and tilted it.

"Enjoying the show, old chum?" asked a deep voice from behind him.

Dropping his bottle, he whirled and reached for his gun, then stopped stock still, the leather only barely cleared. A great big grin spread over his face and he bellowed, "By God! Amos Marple!"

Holstering his gun with a snap, he threw one arm around the tall, blond man, and slapped his back with the other.

Marple, equally pleased, did the same. "It's been eons, Slocum!" he said with a decidedly British accent, once they had gone up the hall and away from the overwhelming sounds of the brawl. "What in the hell are you doing out here in Armpit? I mean, it used to be a decent little mining town, but it's gone down a good bit since I last saw it."

"You're not joshin'," said Slocum, and turned to look at a tossed shot glass, rolling down the hall toward them. "By Christ, it's good to see you, Amos! I came because of a gal."

"That makes sense," said Amos, a grin spitting his tanned and handsome face. He was almost too handsome for his own good, blast him! "They do retain some rather lovely young ladies in this establishment," Amos went on over the shouts and thuds of the brawl behind them. "Well-trained, too. I dare say this brothel is the only thing keeping the town alive."

To their ears came the crash and splinter of glass, and a good deal of it traveled up the stairs. They must've busted one of the front windows, Slocum thought. Or maybe the mirror over the bar.

"That and glass repair," he said.

Slocum watched as, at the end of the hall, a cow-hand stepped onto the upstairs landing, hopped up on the rail, and whooping like a bird, jumped back down into the noisy melee, his arms spread wide.

Slocum turned back to Amos Marple. With a shrug of his shoulders, he said, "It ain't gonna last a whole lot longer at this rate. They're gonna run outta population."

"I concur," Amos said, and put his hand on the latch of number nine. "Care to come in until the fisticuffs die down and they sweep the place out? I have some very fine brandy. And I'd like to talk."

Reminding himself that Tipsy had pretty much disappeared for the duration, Slocum nodded in the affirmative and followed Amos through the door.

He practically walked straight into Tipsy, who was just slipping back into that pink dress—the one that, the last time he'd seen it, had been in a heap on *his* floor.

He scowled and said, "What you doin' in here?"

Tipsy gulped and stammered, "I . . . uh . . . that is, I . . ."

Amos burst out in laughter. In fact, he laughed so hard the he fell into a chair.

"Don't tell me," he finally gasped, "that this is the young lady you came all this way to see? Tipsy, you *are* popular!"

Slocum glared at Amos, and then at Tipsy again. She shrugged. "Sorry, baby. It's . . . it's my job, after all."

And then, flushed with embarrassment, she turned and hurried from the room, half-dressed, and banged the door behind her.

"You know, Slocum, I had to cool my heels for a good hour, waiting for her after I rode in. I can see now whose fault that was!" Amos began to convulse with laughter once more.

And this time, Slocum got caught up in it in spite of himself. He dropped into the chair opposite Amos's and slid his big bare feet up on the low table that stood between them.

Chuckling, he said, "Aw, hell. Tipsy's a soiled dove, after all, and a mighty pretty one. But you know, it never stuck me that she had any admirers other than me. Let alone you!" And then he laughed some more.

Amos got up for a second and brought the cigar box from his nightstand, and an unopened bottle of brandy in its bucket of melting ice. Slocum took a cigar while Amos poured the drinks.

"Havanas," Amos said, still chuckling.

"I know," Slocum said. He bit off the end of his smoke and spat it, long-distance, into a corner of the room. "There's a box in my room, too. Christ, Amos! Same town, same girl . . . what's next, you suppose? If you tell me next that you rode in here on an leopard-colored Appaloosa horse . . ."

Slocum flicked a lucifer into flame and lit his cigar. "Well hell, I might just have to haul off and slug you."

This also delighted Amos no end, for he broke out into a new roar of laughter, nearly spilling the brandy.

But he didn't. He managed to hand Slocum the glass he poured out for him, then take his seat again.

"My dear Slocum," he said, picking up his own glass, "I still favor a solid-colored horse, if you don't mind. None of your loud Paloose horses for me!"

Over the rim of his glass, Slocum said, "All right. Let's keep it that way." He threw Amos a grin. "So what'd you want to see me about? Anything in particular, or it is just gonna be old home week? Not that I mind old home week, long as you keep the brandy flowin'—"

"And the cigars and the women coming," Amos broke in, finishing Slocum's sentence for him.

Actually, that was the single thing about Amos that kind of irritated Slocum. He always felt like Amos was crawling around inside his head.

He just nodded and said, "Right."

Amos drained his glass, then poured out another. He offered the bottle to Slocum, who said, "Not yet." If Amos had to have a couple of drinks to tell him something, it must be a real doozy. And he was beginning to suspect that Amos hadn't been all that surprised to see him.

He sat forward, smoke lazily curling up from his cigar, as he waited.

Abruptly solemn, Amos took another drink of his brandy, staring at his glass as he muttered, "This should have been whiskey."

Slocum waited.

Then Amos looked up.

He said, "You'll forgive me for pretending to be surprised to see you, Slocum. You see, I knew you were coming."

Slocum's eyes narrowed. "You did? How?"

Amos ignored the question and asked one of his own. "You remember the Carthage brothers?"

The cigar, still smouldering, dropped from Slocum's fingers, and he said one word.

"Shit."

2

The Carthage brothers were, indeed, well-known to Slocum.

He and Amos Marple had rounded them up and put them in prison years ago, but not before Amos and Slocum nearly lost their lives. A couple of times.

Rance was the eldest, then Rafe, then Rufus, the baby brother. They all had red hair, but that was where the familial resemblance ended. Their father, who was obviously the redhead in the mix, must have had a roving eye, because all three had different mothers.

Rance Carthage was of medium height, thick-chested with short, massive arms and hands like hams. He had brown eyes and a hell of a temper. It was he who had shot Slocum through the thigh. The slug had barely missed the bone—but not the artery—and if it hadn't been for Amos's fast and expert actions, Slocum would have bled to death. He still had the scar, too.

Rafe, the middle brother, had been birthed by a Mexican mama and although he, too, was redheaded, he had the dark skin and hot temper to prove his ancestry. He was tallish, with eyes as black as flint, and half-crazy. He'd shot Slocum, too, but his bullet had only creased Slocum's skull.

Rafe had taken a bullwhip to Amos, though. Slocum wondered if Amos still bore those whip marks.

He probably did.

Rufus, the youngest of the Carthage boys, had been only seventeen when Slocum and Amos put him and his brothers away. How old would he be now? Twenty-two? Twenty-three, maybe?

Slocum supposed it didn't matter. A jaguar doesn't change his spots, and he doubted that a few years on bread and water in a four-by-six-foot cell had sweetened Rufus's disposition any at all.

The fairest of the three, Rufus was pale-skinned and blue-eyed, and about the same height as his brother, Rafe. Might be some taller, now. Rufus hadn't shot Slocum—not up close and personal, anyway—or come at him with a knife or a whip.

He hadn't done Amos any dirt either, except to fire from a distance. And rig a rope across a rutted road right at chest height, which, when Amos rode into it at a gallop, had knocked him off his horse and knocked him senseless to boot.

But Rufus had committed a far worse crime.

When he rigged that rope tight across the road and they came galloping, hell bent for leather, around the bend, he hadn't counted on Slocum's horse tossing its head in the air at the exact wrong moment.

Slocum still remembered the exact second when old Speck was half-decapitated. Still remembered how he'd run exactly two more strides before he dropped, covering himself and Slocum in a sea of blood. Poor Speck was dead before he hit the ground, probably dead the second that the rope knifed into his jugular.

And Rufus, the little redheaded bastard, had thought it was funny. He'd actually laughed.

Now, Slocum could forgive—or, at least try to forget—a lot of things, but not that, not ever. If the Carthage boys were on the loose, then Rufus was fair game. That was, if Slocum lived through his brothers.

He picked up his cigar before it had a chance to make a hole in the rug, then looked, once again, at Amos. He looked as serious as a heart attack.

Amos said, "They broke out of Yuma about a week ago. They're headed this way."

Slocum's brow creased. "How you know that? You still with the Pinkertons?"

Amos shook his head, then half-smiled. "No, I chose a job with more miserly pay and more danger. You know me. Always looking for a good time. I'm with the Secret Service, now."

"I'll be damned."

"Probably," replied Amos, and sipped at his brandy.

Slocum arched a brow. "What do the Carthage boys have to do with the Secret Service?" he asked. "I thought you boys spent all your time protectin' the president of these United States."

"Most of it," Amos said, crossing his legs and leaning back in his chair. "This is special. We are sent out, from time to time, to deal with local matters that might go national. My current superior—who I shall not name—believes strongly in federal intervention. Legal or not, if you get my drift."

Slocum nodded. "So, you ain't here in an official capacity."

"Correct." Amos paused. "And neither, my friend, are you."

This was getting just a little too convoluted for Slocum to puzzle out, so rather than let it go on any further afield, he said, "What are you sayin', Amos? I ain't a part of this."

Unless that sonofabitch, Rufus, crosses my path, he thought grimly.

"Sorry, but I beg to differ, old chum," Amos said with a perfectly straight face. He placed a hand over his heart. "Your country is calling you."

"No," Slocum said emphatically. He'd already answered his country's call once. He'd joined on the losing side, but that didn't matter to him. Once was enough.

"Oh, yes," Amos went on, unperturbed. "I'm afraid so."

Slocum tossed back the rest of his brandy. "Screw you, Amos." Angrily, he set down his glass. "Why'd you all of a sudden decide to pick on me, anyhow?"

"Because you're the one man I know that I could trust to stand beside me. The one man I know who has the balls to stand up to the Carthage boys. The only one probably still angry enough—and skilled enough."

Slocum scowled. Flattery didn't go far with him, and Amos should know that. He said, "That don't explain how you just happened to bump into me in this lousy, two-bit hole in the wall of a town. Fess up, Amos."

Grinning, Amos leaned over the table and refilled Slocum's glass. "Because," he said, "your life is not so private as you believe it to be."

"Huh?"

"Remember last week, when you stopped for the day in Salt Flats?"

Slocum raised a brow. "Yeah. How in the devil did you know I went through Salt Flats?"

"Do you remember, when you visited the saloon there—the Red Dog Saloon, I believe it was—a short man at a corner table?"

Slocum was getting past testy. He snarled, "No,"

and then said, "How in the hell'd you know I was at the Red Dog?"

"Because of that little man you didn't notice," Amos replied matter-of-factly. "I even know that you ordered three beers over a period of as many hours, won twenty-five dollars at poker, and spent the night with a young lady named Margarita."

Slocum's mouth fell open, but his eyes were narrowed.

Amos continued, "And I suppose you paid no attention to the traveling salesman in the barber shop at Show Low, did you?"

Slocum glared at him.

Amos shrugged his shoulders. "No reason you should. Although they were the same man. Agent, I should say. Your federal government knows a great many details about famous men such as yourself, old chum. Such as where you are going, and on what business."

Spying on him, that's what they were doing! His own damned government was keeping tabs on him!

Slocum got to his feet and growled, "Listen here, Amos, you're a good friend of mine, but I've had about enough of—"

"There, there," Amos said soothingly. "Let me finish. And do have another drink. It's actually fairly decent brandy, considering the vicinity to which it had to be shipped and the abysmal conditions I'm certain it was subjected to."

But Slocum just stood there, scowling, and Amos added, "Please, Slocum. It's important."

Grudgingly, Slocum sat down again and snatched up his glass. "I'm sittin'," he said, and downed his glass in one annoyed gulp. "Hurry up."

Amos sat forward and planted his elbows on his knees. "Listen, my friend. The government has been keeping an eye on you, off and on, for years. They know they have you to thank, among others, for staving off that second rebel war a few years back. They also know that the cavalry wasn't a damn bit of help to you. They know you turned up that despicable serial killer at Three Wives. They know—"

"Sounds like those sonsofbitches know a lot of things," Slocum said curtly. "I say, screw them."

He didn't take to the idea of folks snooping in his private business, not one bit, and he wasn't ashamed to say so.

"But like it or not, Slocum," Amos continued, "screwed or unscrewed, they do know. And when the information came in that those wretched Carthage brothers were headed this way—and that you were, too—well, I'm sorry Slocum, but it was too fateful a coincidence to pass up."

Slocum had a pretty good idea where Amos was going with this, but he said, "What was?"

"Why, for me to meet you here. For the two of us to go up against those bastards again." Amos sat back again and added, quite seriously, "And this time, Slocum, it will be the last time."

"Meaning what?"

"Meaning that we are to act with deadly force," Amos said. "Without prejudice."

"You're sayin' that this time we don't need to haul 'em off to jail?"

"You know as well as I do that they were responsible for the Holworth massacre. Twelve settlers in that group, and they killed them all down to the last woman and child." Amos looked disgusted, and Slocum didn't blame him.

He wished Amos hadn't reminded him, because all he could think of now was finding the plundered wagons, the bodies and among them that little angel of a three-year-old blond girl. Poor baby.

But Amos wasn't done yet. "They emptied two towns of citizens," he went on. "Hazard and Ford's Mill. The ones who didn't flee wished that they had. And the Lord knows what else they've done."

Slocum recalled riding into Ford's Mill with Amos at his side and discovering two men, tied to the paddle wheel of the mill. They had been long dead, white, bloated, and nibbled at by fish.

That, and a ransacked town and a fresh but crude carving on the wall of what had been the mercantile, that read, RUFUS CARTHAGE WAS HERE.

Slocum stiffened. "That was before."

Amos nodded. "Before we put them away, you

mean. If you will recall, the federal authorities thought they should be put to death. Several times over, if possible, and I remember you agreeing . . . well, *strongly* might be too soft a word. It was only because the Arizona Territorial governor at the time was a little . . . softhearted. Modern, he called it, as I remember. Rehabilitation and all that rot."

"More like he was paid off," Slocum rumbled. It still pissed him off, just thinking about it. He looked up, looked Amos right in the eye. "Goddamn lily-livered toad sucker. Come right out with it, Amos. You're tellin' me that this time, we're supposed to kill 'em, aren't you?"

"Unofficially?" Amos said, cocking a brow. "Yes. In other words, no legal action whatsoever will be taken if any or all of the Carthage brothers turn up dead with bullet holes between their shoulder blades. Even if you and I are standing over them with pistols in our hands."

Slocum snorted. "You mean if there happens to be another Federal agent around to stop somebody from hangin' us before we got a chance to explain."

Thoughtfully, Amos scratched his head. "Well, there's that. But this should help."

He dug down into his pocket, pulled out a small, black wallet, and handed it across the table to Slocum. Slocum took it with a raised brow.

"Open it," Amos said.

Slocum did. Inside was an identification card, all

filled out with his name on it. And a badge that read SPECIAL AGENT, UNITED STATES SECRET SERVICE.

"That's only in case of dire emergency, of course," Amos added.

Slocum was silent for a long moment, staring at the damned badge, before he put it down and refilled his own glass. He hated badges, and hated wearing one even worse, but then he thought about that terrible moment with Speck, with the blood washing back over him like somebody had tossed a bucket of it into the air.

And the groan, that terrible, brief strangled groan that Speck had made.

That, and that little blond girl.

Taking a thoughtful puff on his cigar before he drank, he said, "Amos, you're a sonofabitchin' bastard for haulin' me into this. I don't like it. Don't like it at all. But, to put it mildly, I've got even less admiration for the Carthage boys. So you win. I'm in."

"Glad to hear it," Amos said with a crisp nod. He smiled once more. "I thought you'd say that. So drink your drink, then go put on your boots. And your hat. You look odd without it. And then let's go have some dinner. I'm so hungry I could . . . what do you people say out here? I'm so hungry I could eat a mountain lion."

"Bear," Slocum said, standing.

Amos shrugged, and stood up, as well. "Whatever," he said, grinning. "In any case, a large, rather testy, wild animal. Raw."

3

Amos Marple waited a few moments after Slocum left, then stepped out into the hallway to wait for him. They were good friends, he and Slocum, and the fact that Slocum had agreed to help in Amos's pursuit only proved it.

Although they saw each other only every few years, they knew each other like brothers. Well, Amos liked to think so, at any rate.

If it hadn't been for Slocum's dark hair—as opposed to Amos's yellow crop—and their eyes—Slocum's were green, while Amos's were blue—and the fact that Amos had been born in Bath, England, they might well have been kin.

Amos attributed this to a mere accident of birth. He imagined Slocum would have simply snorted derisively if confronted with this theory, however.

Just like good old Slocum, Amos thought with a grin. They were even about the same age, Amos being less than one year Slocum's junior.

"Between the two of us," Amos said softly, "those Carthage boys don't stand a chance."

"You always were an optimistic sonofabitch,"

Slocum said, startling him. He was just coming out his door and settling his hat on his head.

Amos glanced down at Slocum's feet. "Boots. Better. Your feet were a tad gamey, old man."

Slocum grunted. "Nice'a you not to say anything," he growled, "till now."

They started down the hall. It was quiet now, except for the soft sounds of brooms at work floating up the stairs. "Wanna eat here?" Slocum asked.

"I think not," Amos replied as they reached the landing and surveyed the scene below: the aftermath of unbridled and enthusiastic breakage and vandalism. "Food's apt to be laced with broken glass. And the way you eat?" He shook his head. "I'd hate to lose you before we even get started on our quest."

Slocum grumbled, "Goddamn smart ass," but he walked down the stairs. They moved through the bar and out the batwing doors, their boots crunching broken bottles, mugs, windows, and mirrors.

Amos directed them to the Roadrunner Café, the only place in town—besides the saloon—to eat, and they settled in at a corner table, each man taking one of the two chairs that backed to the wall.

Old habits died hard, Amos thought. If Slocum noticed how they'd automatically picked those two exact chairs, he gave no sign of it.

Typical, Amos thought, and gave his head an amused shake.

"Your 16 ounce steak," announced Slocum to the

waiter, who had just appeared. "Charred on the outside," he continued, "and still mooin' on the inside. With all the trimmin's and a side of grilled onions. And apple pie. With cheddar cheese. Oh, and coffee."

Amos didn't even glance at the chalkboard menu. "Same for me," he said amiably. The waiter left before he said, "Hungry, Slocum?"

"Tipsy," was all Slocum said, and Amos understood immediately. The fair Tipsy had given him quite an appetite, too.

But this time, it was for food.

Slocum lit a cigar while they waited for their food. "So why Armpit?" Amos's alter ego asked, once he'd exhaled a plume of smoke. "Why the hell does anybody come to Armpit, except for the whores? And I got a feelin' that those boys took care of their urges about fifteen minutes after they cleared the prison walls."

Amos nodded. Slocum was right on the money, as usual.

He said, "You're correct. They did take care of their urges. They raped a seventeen-year-old girl just outside Yuma, then killed her."

Amos watched as Slocum closed his eyes and lowered his head. He knew it wasn't a prayer. It was anger, pure and simple. Amos remained silent and waited.

He didn't have to wait long before Slocum looked

up, looked at him, and said, "Our killin' 'em is too bright a future for those boys."

"No argument here," Amos said solemnly.

"So why they comin' to Armpit?"

"They're not," Amos said. "They're headed in this general direction, however. I simply swung over this way to—"

"Pick me up," Slocum said, finishing the sentence for him.

Amos smiled. "Precisely."

"When do we leave?"

"Tonight would do nicely, old man."

Slocum scratched at his ear. "Well, Tipsy's glamor has kinda worn off, seein' as how we were plowin' the same field." He shot Amos a look that made him cringe a little. But then Slocum suddenly grinned and added, "But we got time to eat, Mr. Secret Service man?"

"Wouldn't have brought you here if we didn't," Amos replied just as the waiter arrived with a gigantic tray covered with steaming plates.

"Wouldn't have it any other way," Slocum said as the waiter slid a steak in front of him and another in front of Amos. Smothered in grilled onions, the steaks were so huge that they hung over the edges of the plates.

Slocum picked up a knife and a fork. "That's real good, Amos, cause I plan to do a lot of it."

* * *

Roughly forty miles away, the Carthage boys had built themselves a fire, and Rufus, the youngest, was practically up to his armpits in blood. He had been assigned the task of butchering the calf they'd stolen late in the afternoon.

While his brothers, Rance and Rafe, roasted the nicest morsels over the fire, he was stuck carving up most of the rest of the meat into strips, which he was hanging over the bushes to dry, for jerky.

He'd used up all the brush in the vicinity in the process, and was now having to walk about thirty feet away from the fire each time he had a fresh load of beef strips.

"You'd best come out here and help me light another fire," he called to his brothers. "I got a coyote out here that's swipin' our beef."

Rance laughed. "Build it yourself, kid."

"Kill it," Rafe said, without bothering to turn and look at him.

Rufus guessed that Rafe was still ticked off on account of what that barmaid back in the last town had said to him. Rafe hadn't exactly shared her comments with the rest of them, but he'd sure backhanded her into last Tuesday. Knocked out two of her teeth, too.

They'd had to leave town then, Rance had said, on account of Rafe calling attention to them. And when you were wanted for busting out of the territorial prison, you didn't want anyone eyeing you unnecessarily.

Rufus was kind of pissed off about the whole thing. He hadn't even got to order a second beer, let alone finish his first one.

And now he was up to his armpits in fresh blood. It wasn't fair, if you asked him.

He carried the newly carved beef out to the nearest bush—the nearest that had room for it, anyhow— and discovered that his coyote had been back again. He would have shot it the last time, but he couldn't see where it went off to. The land out here was chaparral, thick with scrub.

Good cover for coyotes, bad for riders wanting to keep their beef to themselves.

He hung out the strips, draping them carefully over the branches so that they'd dry even, and then he went even farther out into the scrub to gather firewood. He piled the wood wide and high, always listening carefully for the hiss of a rattlesnake, and every once in a while yelling to spook the unseen coyote away.

Then Rufus, still as red as a painted Indian, dug a circle around the pile with his boot heel, going over it several times to make sure it was wide enough. There wasn't any wind, but you had to be careful about things like fires, and thus he made the marginal firebreak anyway.

Only then did he kneel down to where some of

his kindling brush protruded beneath the ironwood, mesquite, and palo verde limbs, and proceed to strike a match into flame.

When he was satisfied that the fire was burning bright and that the coyote hadn't come to call again, he went back to business.

Except that the carcass wasn't there anymore. He saw the draw-marks where it had been hauled through the dust and off into the brush, saw the coyote tracks, half-hidden by the carcasses trail, and sighed.

Well, hell. He was tired of butchering beef, anyhow.

"Rance?" he said as he ambled toward the fire. "Toss me that canteen, would you?"

Chewing, Rance tossed it over.

Rufus began washing his arms and chest down. The blood was already drying and getting sticky. "You better have saved me some'a that rib meat," he said, scrubbing at his elbow.

Rafe finally looked back at him and, straight-faced, said, "Aw, gee, kid. Did you have your little ol' heart set on that?"

Scowling, Rufus stopped scrubbing. "You better not have et my meat after I butchered that whole damn calf all by my lonesome!"

Rance spoke up. "Aw, don't go gettin' your knickers in a knot, baby brother. And Rafe, shut up.

Your meat's over here, Rufus. I saved it aside before the Mexican pig-boy could get to it."

Rufus watched stoically while Rafe dropped his plate in the dirt and went roaring after the far more brutishly built Rance, his arms outstretched.

"How many times I gotta tell you, you stupid sonofabitch?" Rafe hollered as he grabbed Rance's throat with both hands. "Don't go callin' me a Mex!"

Despite the death-grip that would have throttled any other man, Rance laughed. "But you are, Rafe," he said as he almost effortlessly pried loose his brother's fingers. "You are."

Before Rafe could get a new grip on him, Rance simply shoved Rafe down to the ground. Rufus, half-washed, shook his head. By Christ, that Rance was one strong son of a buck!

Rafe landed with a thud, and as Rance sat himself back down, he said, "I'm gonna tell you again, brother. See, my mama was a Hungarian—that good, hardy, peasant stock, Daddy used to say. Little Rufus, here, had a Scot for a mama—"

"Don't call me little," Rufus protested. "I'm taller'n both'a you."

"And I already know who my mama was, you goddamn badger's butt," grumbled Rafe. "I'm tired of hearin' you repeat this every time we—"

"And you, Rafe, were out of a Mex woman," Rance went on, nonplussed. "Get used to it. You go round jumping everybody that calls you what you look like—well, except for that red mop of yours—you're gonna have to battle your way through the whole of the U.S. of A."

"He already slugged his way through most of Yuma prison," Rufus said diplomatically as he shrugged back into his shirt. It clung to his still-damp skin in places, and turned pinkish at the spots he hadn't washed very well.

"Damn right, I did," Rafe said. His words were surly, but his obsidian eyes flashed with pride.

The best way to calm down old Rafe, Rufus knew, was to compliment him on how many folks he'd either beat to squash or sent home to Jesus.

Rufus squatted down on Rance's far side, then took the plate Rance held toward him. He picked up the rack of bones, pulled off a long, single rib and took a bite. It was tender to the tooth and juicy with fat.

"Good," he said, nodding and chewing. "Real damned good."

"Should be," said Rance, attention on his own plate. "Fixed it extra special, kinda spicy." He shrugged, then nodded toward Rafe. "Had the Mex, here, piss on it before I put it on the fire."

A new fistfight broke out, this one three-sided.

Slocum and Amos Marple left Armpit—as well as a sniffling Tipsy Magee—behind when the moon was high and the stars were bright. However, there was enough light that they were able to travel the old stage road at a slow jog.

"So where you figure these boys are?" Slocum asked, once they were a mile or two out of town. He figured they could get a good two or three hours of riding in before the clouds on the horizon moved in to cover what moon there was. "I mean, you know exactly or anything? You got people followin' me all over hell and gone. Shouldn't be too much trouble to follow three sidewinders like the Carthage boys."

Amos made a tut-tut sound and shook his head. "So facetious, Slocum? Why, I would have thought that was beneath you."

Slocum snorted. "Stop tryin' to change the subject, Amos."

Amos tipped his head in resignation. "Yes, we have had someone on them. At a safe distance."

"And what's that?" Slocum asked. "Seems to me like the safest distance is somewhere in New Jersey."

Amos snorted this time, but there was a laugh in it. He said, "True, true. The last report, which I received just before I went to visit the lovely Miss Tipsy, puts them in open country, approximately halfway between Harrington City and Mescalero. Give or take."

"And we're just supposed to ride right on up to

'em," Slocum said flatly. "Say, 'howdy, there, boys,' and shoot 'em. Gotta say, Amos, I like your optimism. Don't trust it worth a damn, but I like it. Looks good on you. Really."

"Slocum?" Amos said.

"What?"

"Shut up."

Slocum shrugged and grinned a little, all while staring straight ahead at the road. In his whole life, only two people—that he'd let live, anyhow—had told him to shut up.

One was Amos Marple.

Hell, usually folks were raggin' on him to say something, say *anything!*

He got a real kick out of Amos.

He had a feeling that he was going to get a kick out of finding the Carthage brothers, too, but it'd be in a far more literal sense. He wasn't looking forward to that part, but he *was* looking forward to finally ridding the Southwest of those vermin for good and all.

The cloud bank had moved closer much faster than he'd thought it would, he realized. It was also looking a good bit more threatening.

Once again, Amos read his mind and said, "Maybe another hour before we camp, old chum? I don't like the look of those clouds."

"Dammit, Amos," Slocum growled. "If I'd known this was comin', I would'a stayed over another night in Armpit. With a woman. Any woman."

Amos snorted. "As would I. But look on the bright side, Slocum. They're only clouds. Not rain."

Exactly one half hour later, they were squatted beneath Amos's tented blanket while white, pea-sized pellets of hail pelted into the desert around them, melting almost immediately into the hot, hard, gravelly soil.

"Well, it's not rain," Amos said cheerily.

"Shut up, Amos," grumbled Slocum.

4

The next morning at first light, Rufus Carthage woke to find that both fires had gone out, and all his carefully carved up jerky was gone, too. There were prints of coyotes—or maybe just one very busy coyote—all over the area.

Fuming, he kicked his brothers awake.

"Why didn't you tend the damned fires!" he demanded of Rance, who was rubbing his eyes. "You was supposed to be on guard!"

"What the hell are you babblin' about?" was all Rance said.

"And you were supposed to be on watch before him!" Rufus carried on, giving the slower-to-wake Rafe a hard kick in the shins.

Rafe simply grunted and rolled over.

Rance sat up and threw his blanket aside. "Just what the devil are you grousin' about now, kid?"

"My goddamn meat, that's what!" Rufus shouted. "It's been took! The goddamn coyotes took it 'cause you and Rafe didn't feed the fires!"

Rance rolled his eyes and lifted his sizable bulk

up off the ground. "Don't matter," he said, dusting off his knees.

"What you mean, it don't matter?" Rufus roared. "Why else did you have me carvin' up that calf half the night?" He was steaming mad now. His neck and face were hotter than a stove lid, and his ears weren't far behind.

"Aw, hell, kid, we was just tryin' to keep you busy," Rance said as he picked up his bedroll. "Rafe, you gonna sleep the morning away, you lazy slug?"

"Might," Rafe grumbled from beneath his blankets. "If you two'd shut the hell up."

But Rufus, not one to let things go by, demanded, "What the hell you mean, keep me busy? I had blood all over me, goddamn it! You know I hate butcherin'."

From the ground, Rafe barked out a laugh. "Only up close, as I remember. You sure did a job on that feller's horse."

"What feller?" Rufus half shouted.

"One'a the ones what brought us in," Rufus said. He finally lowered his blanket and sat up, puffy-faced. "You know, years ago. What's his name?"

"Slocum," answered Rance. He was on his knees, relighting their campfire.

"Shut up," Rufus said. They were trying to confuse him again, and he didn't appreciate it.

Rafe dumped the contents of a canteen into their

coffeepot, then threw in some Arbuckle's and handed it to Rance.

Rance set it on the infant fire, then looked up at Rufus. "Because you're too damn full of it, kid. We was just givin' you somethin' to do to take the edge off. Why, hell, I figured that if we didn't keep you busy, you were bound to cornhole old Rafe in his sleep."

Strangely enough, Rufus burst out laughing, although Rafe didn't look too pleased at the idea.

"Reckon you're right, there, Rance," Rufus said. "I didn't get me near enough'a that gal before you two idiots decided to kill her. Gal's no good for nothin' when she's dead."

"Tell that to Rafe," Rance said, and the darker skinned brother glowered at him.

"If it wasn't so early and I wasn't so tired," Rafe said, "I'd beat you into next week, Rance."

Rance just smiled. "Don't worry, boys," he said. "In a couple of days, we're gonna have a whole town all to ourselves. And I'll bet that some of the population is female."

Rufus grinned.

That morning after the hailstorm—which was followed by a hammering rain that had lasted perhaps five minutes before it passed over them—Slocum and Amos Marple were on the trail once more.

Such odd weather, Amos thought. *I shall never grow accustomed to it.*

Today had dawned as hot, if a little more sultry, than yesterday, and they hadn't made much distance previously because of the storm.

Lord, it had been loud! Such booming and crashing! For a little while there, Amos had been sure that he'd be struck by a bolt of lightning, and Slocum would be left with a flash-fried companion for the hunt.

But he wasn't, and therefore, they went on.

What slayed him was that Slocum had stayed so blasted calm through the entire process. He was more accustomed to such things, Amos imagined. Amos himself only came this far west when duty called.

In fact, for the last three years, he'd been shuffling paper in an office in Washington, D.C. He'd leapt at the chance to take this assignment, even though it should have gone to a junior associate.

The fact was that he missed active duty. He missed the thrill of it. He missed the rush of adrenaline when he was riding hard, and he missed the exquisite high of the capture.

Learning that Slocum was in the neighborhood had sealed it. The two of them, together, had put the Carthage boys in prison once before, and they would do it again. Although this time, it would be in the cemetery at Yuma or someplace else rather than in a cell.

And he'd missed Slocum. Missed his silences and his taciturn streak, missed his confidence. Most of all, he'd missed the company of a man who was really . . . well . . . a man. Slocum brought out Amos's own best side. And he needed that right at the moment. He'd been feeling a little too much like a clerk, too much like a cog in a wheel.

For probably the last time, he would be a field agent. He'd have an active part.

He was enjoying the chase already.

"Do you *have* to hum all the goddamn time?" Slocum groused.

"Sorry, old chum," Amos said. "Just feeling my oats, I expect. I was just thinking how lovely it was to be actually working on a case again. Other than reading the reports from other agents, I mean, and making those grand executive decisions."

"Well, put an executive stopper in it," Slocum said. And then he allowed a smile to quirk up one corner of his mouth. "Either that, or hum somethin' besides 'The Rose of Tralee.' It's wearin' thin."

Amos smiled. "Your wish is my command. Perhaps you'd prefer something more American. " 'Streets of Laredo,' perhaps? 'Yankee Doodle Dandy'?"

"Not that last one," Slocum said quickly.

"Sorry, I forgot," Amos said. "You were on the opposing side, weren't you?"

Slocum sighed. "Do we gotta talk about this?"

Amos shrugged, and held his peace.

Just as well, Slocum thought, his gaze on the trail ahead. He figured they could stay on this road for maybe another three miles before they'd have to veer off to the south.

That was, if Rufus, Rafe, and Rance were headed the way Amos said they were. Although how in the hell Amos expected him to find them in the middle of nowhere was a mystery. Amos must think he had a nose like a bloodhound or something.

But Slocum *did* know that there was only one town they could be headed for, considering their route. If they were going to stop over in a town, it would have to be a little wide spot in the road called Hoopskirt.

Hoopskirt had no telegraph, it wasn't on the stage route, and it had probably less than two hundred inhabitants if you counted the surrounding ranchers and their help. There were likely less than seventy-five people living in the town, proper.

The Carthage boys could cut quite a swath through a town like that, and be long gone before anybody heard about it.

So his money was on Hoopskirt.

Besides, he didn't figure the Carthage brothers would be able to go too long without tearing up something. They'd only killed that one poor little seventeen-year-old gal, which for them was the same as a normal man downing a casual beer. They were probably reaching the end of their tether, mayhem-wise.

They were due for a real bender.

In the sleepy little town of Hoopskirt, Sheriff Robert "Blue" Parker sat out on his office porch in his rocker, carefully whittling what was supposed to be a house finch and taking in the morning sun.

Folks called him Blue for one of two reasons. The first was that his own eyes were a sort of pale, uncanny turquoise, made even more startling by the dark fringe of lashes that surrounded them.

The second reason was that, because his eyes were sensitive to the harsh Arizona sun, he'd had a pair of special glasses made for himself: dark blue glass, no correction.

He wore them most all the time when he was outside. Sometimes when he was inside, too. And he'd worn them—or other pairs, just like them—for as long as he could remember.

Most folks didn't even know his real first name was Robert, which suited him fine. Well, mostly, he just didn't give a rat's ass.

He'd landed this cozy perch several years back, and it sure as hell beat saddle-bumming and bounty hunting all over hell and gone, and looking for work

that wasn't there. Course, the job didn't pay worth
a damn, but he had a little saved by. He had his own
little house, and a woman who came in once a week
to tidy up.

It was enough, and there certainly wasn't much
danger of his getting killed.

There wasn't even much danger of his getting a
splinter, when you got right down to it. There
weren't many places any quieter than Hoopskirt.

"Sheriff Parker?" a voice called from inside the
office. "Blue, you out there?"

"Yeah, Frank," he called in reply, without looking up from his whittling. He was having a little
trouble with the feathers on the wings. "What?"

"Come an' help me. This damned drawer's stuck
again."

Lazily, Sheriff Blue Parker stood and brushed the
wood shavings from his britches. Frank and his
lousy file drawers.

Well, actually, it'd probably be the most exciting
thing to happen this week. Hoopskirt was damned
dull, Blue thought as he walked through the door
and into the jail's office.

But it was a nice kind of dull.

"Bird looks to be comin' along nice," Frank commented. He was as chubby and short as Blue was
tall and lean. At the moment, he had both hands
locked firmly around the edge of a file cabinet, and
his eyes locked on the piece of wood in Blue's hand.

"Yeah," Blue replied, and set the wooden finch on the desk. "How many times I got to remind you, Frank? You gotta unlock the blasted thing before you try to get it open."

Suddenly sheepish, Frank muttered, "Oh, yeah," and let go of the cabinet long enough to open a desk drawer. He pulled out a skeleton key. "Sorry, Blue," he said. "Forgot."

"Again," Blue replied. He sat down behind his desk and put his feet up, then took off his glasses and set them on the desktop. Everything swam from shades of blue back into full color again. "Anything up for today?" he asked.

"Well," said Frank, this time opening the afore-mentioned cabinet with ease, "Mrs. Goodwell's cat, Fluffy, has got up that big ol' cottonwood in the yard again and can't get down. Told her I'd be along around ten, if he hasn't hit the ground by hisself yet."

Blue, who was reading new wanted poster from the pile on his desk, nodded sagely. "Wear gloves this time, Frank. You know Fluffy always claws the bejesus out of you."

"If I can remember." Frank pulled a brown paper package out of the drawer, then closed it again. He handed Blue the key, which Blue dropped back in its desk drawer, then unwrapped the package, producing two ham and mustard sandwiches. He handed one to Blue.

"Breakfast?" he asked.

"Soon as the coffee's ready," Blue said. Shoving the paper away—no outlaws ever came here, *nobody* ever came here. He leaned back and closed his eyes.

"Dagnabit!" he heard Frank say. "I knowed I forgot to do somethin'!"

By nightfall, Slocum and Amos again made camp. There was another cloud bank on the horizon, and Slocum wasn't taking any chances. He found a nice stand of rock with a wide overhang, and parked both them and the horses beneath it.

As he built a fire near the edge of the outcrop, Amos said, "Slocum, you haven't said a word this entire day about where we're going. We are on the correct path, aren't we?"

Slocum grunted. "Sort of. Plan to outflank 'em. We're headed for Hoopskirt."

Amos thought this over for a moment. "Hoopskirt?" he finally asked. "Don't believe I'm familiar with it."

"Sleepy town, not much in the way of population. It's on their way if they keep on goin' the way they've been. No telegraph or train, let alone stagecoach. Just the kind'a place they'd like to shoot up."

Amos nodded. "Knew I could count on you, old boy."

"That and four bits'll buy you a shot of whiskey,"

Slocum said, smirking into the fire, which was just coming to life. He gave it a stir, and a little flurry of sparks rose up into the air.

"Is there any chance that we might beat them there?" Amos asked.

Slocum shrugged. "Dunno. We might make it tomorrow night, but I don't know how far along they are, or whether they're dawdlin'." He was pretty sure he knew where Amos was going with that question, but did nothing to draw it out of him.

As it turned out, he didn't have to. Amos said, "I hope to God we do. I don't want the blood of another town on my hands."

Slocum twisted toward him. "Always takin' the blame, ain't you, Amos? You didn't hack down the population of those towns five years ago. The Carthage brothers did that all by themselves."

"True. But I should have been there sooner. I could have stopped it. I tell you, Slocum, those poor dead people haunt my dreams."

Slocum sighed. Amos was suddenly depressed, as down as Slocum had ever seen him. For a happy-go-lucky sort like Amos, this wasn't a good sign.

Slocum was tempted to say, *Well, stop dreamin' then, you limey idiot.*

But instead, he said, "Amos, you caught 'em. You and me. And we kept 'em from doin' it again. And again. And again. See, I figure we saved a lot of lives, not the other way round."

Amos didn't look at Slocum. Apparently he was in one of his rare pensive moods, and he just stared out over the open plain in silence.

Slocum let him be.

5

At a little after two o'clock the next afternoon, Sheriff Blue Parker was standing on a chair in his office, sinking a nail to hang a picture. The Widow Jenks had given it to him as a gift, and he figured he couldn't rightly turn it down, even if the Widow was sweet on him and he wasn't sweet on her.

It would be bad manners.

So he decided to hang it in the office, on the wall behind his desk where he wouldn't have to look at it much. It was a print of a racehorse, and he actually kind of liked it.

Too bad it had come from the Widow Jenks.

His office wall displayed several similar objects from the town's female population. There was a wooden plaque carved with a crude, three-dimensional picture of a barn with two trees from Megan Spivey, a hand-painted wooden tray with a big rooster in the middle of it from the elderly Miss Kelly at the mercantile, a cuckoo clock all the way from Switzerland from the relatively wealthy Widow Frankenthaler and so on.

His wall was getting crowded. If women kept insisting of giving him things, he wished they'd stick to baked goods or fried chicken. At least a man could eat those and send the plate back. And Hoop-skirt seemed to have more than its share of good cooks.

Now, Blue wasn't immune to the charms of women. He had once loved a woman with all his heart and soul. But diphtheria had taken her away to Jesus, along with his unborn child. He still spoke to his Janey when things got tough. He liked to think that she heard him from her perch up there in heaven.

And although, every once in a while, he availed himself of one of the gussied up gals over at Billing's Saloon, he had no intention of marrying again. He was a man who could love, and love truly, only once in a lifetime.

The nail having been sunk, he took the print off the top of the filing cabinets and hung it, playing with it until it hung even, then climbed down off the chair. He was just returning it to its place on the opposite side of the room when Frank came barreling in, panting and gasping for breath.

"Whoa, whoa!" Blue said, and caught the shorter man by the shoulders. "What'd you do, run all the way from Ashley's farm or somethin'?"

"It's . . . it's . . ." Frank couldn't catch his breath long enough to get more than a word out.

Blue waited.

And finally, haltingly, Frank said, "It's Tom Crisp. Somebody's killed him, Blue, just killed him while he was sittin' out on the front stoop of his porch."

"Who told you that?" Blue asked. The Crisp place was several miles out of town. Hell, maybe Frank had run from there?

But Frank said, "Arvil Roman, Tom's ramrod. Said it was three fellas—all with red hair—and that nobody'd ever seen before. Said they took off the minute they seen Arvil and some of the other boys runnin' up from the barn."

Blue stiffened. "They chasin' 'em?"

Frank nodded. "Arvil said they pretty much lost 'em up in the rocks, but Harry and Dutch are still out there, lookin'. Arvil caught me down at the edge of town, then he took off again."

Frank finally collapsed in the chair that Blue had dragged halfway across the room, and put his head in his hands. "Poor Tom!" he cried. "Just sitting out on his front stoop!"

But Blue dragged him to his feet again. "C'mon, Frank. We gotta get out there and see what this is about."

"Well, Blue, it's about they killed Tom Crisp! Ain't you been listenin'?"

Blue closed his eyes for a moment, then opened them and said, "I know that, Frank. What we got to do is go out there and catch 'em, and maybe find out *why*. Bring 'em to justice. See?"

"Oh," said Frank. His hands were still shaking. "Oh."

"That's it, Frank," Blue said as he snatched his colored glasses off the desk, crammed them on his face, and headed Frank toward the door.

Poor Frank. But he was the best the town had to offer in the way of a deputy. Blue figured that as sad as Frank could be sometimes, he was a whole lot better than nothing.

They were out on the street and headed toward the livery when Blue suddenly stopped dead in his tracks. Frank went on a couple paces before he stopped and turned around.

"What?" he asked. His face was still ashen.

Blue took pity on him. "Been thinkin', Frank."

" 'Bout what?"

" 'Bout how you'd best stay in town," Blue said. Relief flooded into Frank's face instantly, and Blue knew he'd made the right decision. "You go round and tell folks what happened. Tell 'em to be on their guard, just in case. Chances are those boys had a grudge against Tom Crisp for some reason, but it's better to be safe than sorry."

"That's right, Blue," Frank said, nodding. "That's sure right."

"I want you to stay here and watch the town while I try to run down Arvil and his boys," Blue said. "Hell, maybe they already got them fellers. But you see any strangers ridin' in? Don't shoot, don't ask questions, just get everybody the hell inside."

Blue wouldn't put it past Frank to shoot a bullet in the general direction of just about anybody, in the state he was in. He didn't want Frank killing off— or, more likely, scaring to death—some traveling preacher or cattle buyer.

"Got you, Sheriff," Frank said.

"Well, go on," Blue barked with a roll of his eyes, which he'd learned long ago that nobody could see when he had his glasses on. "Get goin'."

"Right, Blue," Frank said, "I'll do it right now!" and took off toward Jensen's café. Hopefully, to spread the word.

Blue trotted on down to the livery and quickly tacked up Crackerjack, his strawberry roan gelding. Now, Blue was a good deal more concerned than he'd let on to Frank. This was a quiet town, a town where nothing much happened except cats up trees or the occasional kid's prank. Blue was a handy man with a gun—or he had been, at one time—but the days of his bounty hunting were long past.

He wondered just what the hell he'd do if these men were handier, or faster. Or younger, which they undoubtedly were. Seemed like everybody was younger than him these days.

He led Crackerjack out of the stable, mounted up, and set off down Main Street at a lope. Whatever sort of shape his skills were in, he supposed he was about to find out.

Slocum and Amos had ridden at a good pace and without incident, and ambled into Hoopskirt along about six o'clock that evening, when the sun was just nearing the horizon. They'd made good time, better than the last time Slocum had been here.

Of course, that time he'd had Horseface Malone and a couple of rustlers in between himself and the town, and Horseface and his boys objected to the direction Slocum was coming.

He'd been right happy to haul them in, once he'd got a few ropes around them.

He wasn't so happy about what he and Amos found this afternoon, though.

The streets were empty of people. Hoopskirt was a quiet town, but not this quiet. At the livery, the hostler said not a word, but bolted out the back door when they led their horses in.

"Was it something we said?" Amos asked as he led his gelding into a vacant stall.

"Don't know," Slocum replied. He lifted the saddle from Sonny's back. "Didn't give us a chance to say anything."

"Well, at least we beat the Carthage boys here," Amos said hopefully, although Slocum noticed that he kept one eye on the door as he measured out grain for the horses. "There aren't nearly enough bodies in the streets for them to have arrived."

Slocum snorted. "These folks are scared of some-thin', though. Wish I knew what it was."

Quickly, he ran a brush over Sonny, his freckle-nosed Appaloosa gelding. Sonny was sort of an odd-looking Appy, being a palomino with a white blanket over his golden rump and golden, thumb print-sized spots on the blanket. Slocum liked the way he looked, though.

"Sorry, boy," he said, in apology for the lick-and-a-promise grooming.

He left four bits on the top of a barrel to pacify the hostler, if and when he ever came back and, to the sound of horses contentedly crunching grain, he and Amos took their leave of the stable.

They walked out, once again, into the vacant street. There wasn't the slightest sight or sound of human habitation in the place. No kids yelling, no piano music or rowdy-dow from the saloon, no faint jingling of harness or plod of a hoof, no sound of a sweeping broom, not even the scuff of a boot.

Despite the heat, Amos rubbed at his arms. "I feel as if someone just walked over my grave. It's bleed-ing eerie, Slocum."

"Yeah," Slocum replied grimly as he headed to-ward the saloon, eyes flicking quickly from building to building, alley to alley, doorway to doorway.

One hand rested gently on the butt of his gun.

Amos followed, in much the same manner.

•   •   •

Blue couldn't find anybody.

Couldn't even find a trace of a track, once he trailed everybody to the place where the rock started. He'd been going around in circles for some time, trying to find any trace that he could latch onto, but hadn't come up with anything.

Resignedly, he turned his roan toward town again. He hadn't seen anybody, but at least he hadn't heard any shots either. Sound carried fairly well out here, and he was halfway confident that Arvil and the rest of the late Tom Crisp's boys hadn't found anything either. Which meant that they probably hadn't come to any harm.

He hoped.

He had ridden perhaps half a mile when he topped a breast of land and practically rode right into Arvil Roman, along with Harry Jones and Dutch Wheeler.

In fact, Arvil had his gun drawn before they recognized each other.

"Sheriff," he said with a tired nod, and holstered his gun. He and the other two were off their weary horses. Harry and Dutch didn't even bother to get up from the ground. They just nodded at him and continued mopping their brows.

"Horses look all in," Blue said.

"We put a fair number of miles under 'em," Arvil

said, and took off his hat just long enough to run a dirty sleeve over his brow.

"You catch sight of the bastards?" Blue asked.

"Nothin'," spat Dutch, from the ground. "Not a goddamn thing."

Harry just shook his head.

"Who's takin' care of Tom?" Blue asked, keeping his voice as level as he could. He'd liked old Tom Crisp, and he knew these boys had been devoted to him.

"Young Trey's seein' to him," Arvil replied, then sneered. "He stayed back. In case those evil sonsofbitches came back again, he'll blow 'em to Kingdom Come, you'll see."

Seeing as "Young Trey," Tom Crisp's grandson, was only sixteen, Blue had his doubts that the boy could best anybody in a gunfight, but withheld his comment.

Instead, he asked, "You know any reason why anybody'd have a grudge against old Tom?"

All three men shook their heads no, and the so far silent Harry said, "Y'know, I knowed Tom for maybe fifteen, sixteen years. Didn't nobody have a little dislike for him, let alone a strong one." Then he added, "Don't get me wrong, Blue. He could be a hard man in business."

The other two nodded.

"But he were always fair," Harry finished.

"That's true, Harry," Blue said sympathetically.

"I never met a feller had even a harsh word against him. I'm right sorry for your loss. The whole town'll miss Tom Crisp."

"What you gonna do, Blue?" Arvil asked, and Blue knew that one question contained about sixteen others.

He sighed and said, "I'm gonna ride back to town, Arvil. I been lookin' since you rode in to tell Frank, and I ain't turned up nothin' either. Guess I'm gonna get the town locked up good and tight for the night, then get together a posse in the morning."

He didn't add that what posse he'd be able to turn up in Hoopskirt was slim to none, and on top of that, he had no idea where he'd be leading them. But he figured he had to say something, if only to put these boys' minds at ease, let them know he was trying to do something, anything.

He added, "After your horses get rested up a bit, you boys head on home. I'll expect you in town come first light, though."

Arvil nodded brusquely. "Ain't nothin' that could keep us away, Blue."

"Right," said Harry.

"You betcha," added Dutch.

Blue tipped his hat, then rode back toward Hoopskirt. He hoped he could come up with a better plan by morning. And he also hoped that those killers had steered clear of town and gone on their way.

6

Slocum and Amos pushed through the batwing doors of Hoopskirt's only saloon to find exactly four men in the place: the bartender, who was shaking so hard he was about to drop the glass he was pretending to polish, and three customers, each one at a different table, and each one white as a sheet.

All four of them were staring at Slocum and Amos.

"Good afternoon, fellows," Amos said cheerily, and tipped his hat.

"A-afternoon, gents," stuttered the barkeep.

Slocum sauntered over to the bar, his gaze flicking from one parchment-colored customer to the next. "Couple'a beers," he said.

Amos came and stood on his left, leaving enough room between them that Amos could clear leather and fire quickly. And also enough room, Slocum noted, that Amos could turn immediately toward the door, if need be, and fire, leaving the rest of the saloon for Slocum to take care of.

Again, Slocum thought what a handy bastard Amos was to have around.

The barkeep brought their beers, and set them down with shaking hands. Slocum clapped a hand on the man's wrist before he had a chance to move away.

"Mind tellin' me why everybody in this town's so nervous?" he asked. He and Amos had been keeping an eye peeled for any sign of the Carthage boys, and there wasn't any. Unless they were sending somebody ahead to warn the town they were about to invade, which was highly unlikely. This just didn't make any sense.

"Everybody n-nervous?" asked the bartender, his voice quavering. "D-don't know why you'd s-say that, m-mister."

Slocum let go of his wrist, and the man practically leapt back to the far end of the bar, knocking over a tray of shot glasses in his haste.

They clattered to the floor, and the other startled customers jumped, one clean out of his chair.

"Slocum?" Amos said softly, and Slocum turned to see a new fellow entering the saloon. He was of medium height, dark-haired, exceedingly nervous-looking, and he was wearing a deputy's badge on his vest.

"Finally," Slocum said, and turned toward him. "What the hell's going on around here, any—"

Something hit him, slammed into the back of his head, and the whole world went black.

●   ●   ●

The Carthage boys sat their horses on a low ridge to the north, while Rufus took his turn with Rafe's binoculars.

They had lost their pursuers earlier and easily, and had circled wide around the town. Now they viewed it from the opposite direction of the place where Rafe had shot the old rancher off his rocking chair.

It had been a real whizzer of a shot, Rufus thought, and he had won three dollars on it. Rance had handed it over grudgingly, once they lost those riders and were in the clear again.

"I'm tellin' you, it was just a mistake, that's all," Rance had said while he dug for the money. "Rafe ain't never shot that good before. He must'a been aimin' for the barn."

Rufus had ducked out of the way in time to avoid Rafe's fist, and just in time to snatch the three bucks out of Rance's hand.

Well, that Rafe, he just wouldn't learn. Now one of his flint-black eyes was starting to turn purple, and his nose was all swollen. Served him right, Rufus thought.

Rance wasn't only the best shot in the family, but you went into a fistfight with him knowing that you'd be beat to a pulp. That was just the way it was.

Which was why Rufus avoided making his oldest brother mad.

"Anything goin' on down there?" Rafe asked.

"Looks like the sheriff's draggin' a couple of fellers off to the jail," Rufus said, watching through the binoculars as four men, one with a tiny, dull glint of tin on his chest, dragged two senseless men through the street, then into the jail.

"They got a sheriff these days?" Rance asked, and reached for the binoculars. "Gimme those," he said as he snatched them from Rufus's hands and raised them to his own eyes. "They didn't last time I was through here."

"He ain't out there anymore," Rufus said. "He went in the jail."

"We gonna ride down or what?" Rafe asked, tentatively fingering his swollen nose. "I want me a woman, and I want her all night, by God."

"Good thing they got a whorehouse," Rance quipped, still staring through the lenses at the quiet town below. And then he added, with a snort, "You're too ugly to get you a woman for free."

Rafe leaned toward him, and his brother Rance, never moving, said, "You want me to match them eyes up for you, Rafe?"

Rafe sat back and crossed his wrists over his saddle horn. "Shittin' bastard," Rufus heard him mumble.

It beat anything, the way his older brothers argued and fought all the time. Rufus somehow thought that, as a rule, brothers ought to get along.

They did in other families. Just not his, he guessed. Why, even in Yuma there'd been a few sets of brothers, and they got along just fine. Sort of.

His didn't, though. For his part, he simply tried to be agreeable and stay out of the middle when they started throwing punches. Heck, they were fun to be around when they got going on somebody other than each other. He really enjoyed their company, then.

One of the finest times in his young life was when they'd torn up that town just over the border, in Nevada. Damn, that had been fine!

And now they were about to do it again.

Rufus, all of twenty-three years old—seven of which had been spent in assorted jails and prisons—looked down at the town, laying before them like a ripe plum, plump and juicy and waiting to be picked and eaten.

Unconsciously, he licked his lips.

Slocum came around slowly, and with one hell of a headache.

And also, he was surrounded by bars.

He didn't sit up yet. He took a moment to figure out what was going on, and how the devil he'd gotten there. He came up with nothing, except that the damned bartender must have slammed him in the skull with something from behind.

The man must have dealt Amos a blow, too. He

could see him on a second cot, across the cell, out like the proverbial light.

And, between his feet and beyond the bars, he saw that lame-ass, sonofabitch deputy sitting smugly behind a desk.

Slowly, holding his throbbing head, Slocum sat up. The deputy looked over at the first sign of Slocum's movement, and though Slocum was safely behind the bars and no longer armed, the deputy recoiled. So violently, in fact, that he shoved his chair clear back against the wall.

He's plenty scared, Slocum thought. *Maybe the Carthage boys are here already.*

But then he decided no. If the Carthage boys were in town, the first shots they'd take would be at anybody wearing a badge. And this fellow looked like the type that would have run for the hills if anybody'd shot at him and missed.

"What the hell are you so jumpy about?" was the first thing out of Slocum's mouth. "Why are we in here, and what the hell's wrong with this town?"

The deputy blanched some, but distance and a locked iron door made him brave enough to say, "Like you don't know, you cowardly murderers! Tom Crisp was a good man, and a pillar of this here community. Shame on you."

That last phrase, with words so tame, was practically spat out hard enough to make them the foulest curse.

Slocum scowled. "Don't know what you're talkin' about, deputy. Where's your boss? And who the hell's Tom Crisp?"

Under the guise of scratching his leg, Slocum felt for his boot knife, and discovered that they hadn't found it.

He still had it, safe and secure. And if worse came to worse, he'd use it.

The deputy pressed his lips together. He wasn't talking anymore.

"Fine," muttered Slocum, and rose. He went over to Amos's cot, saw that he was breathing, his chest rising and falling regularly, and said, "Amos? Amos! Wake up, man!"

When that didn't work, he picked up the wash bucket from the floor and upended it over Amos's face.

Amos came to with a sputter. First thing, he reached for his gun, which wasn't there, then he looked up at Slocum, blinking.

"What the devil's going on?" he asked. He brushed water from his eyes. "And why did you feel called upon to do that?"

"Cause you were out cold, that's why," Slocum said, then nodded toward the deputy. "Tried askin' him why we're in here, but he ain't talkin'."

In reply, the deputy crossed his arms, as if to lock himself even further away from his prisoners.

"Are we still in Hoopskirt?" Amos asked, flicking

water from his face and hair. He glanced down toward the empty pail. "And did you feel the absolute need to use the *entire* bucket?"

With a sniff, Slocum sat down on his own cot again. "Seemed like a good idea at the time." He twisted toward the deputy, who was still standing, arms crossed, his back against the wall, which was covered by all matter of things that seemed out of place in the town jail.

Slocum didn't mention it, though. "It's dark out," he said. "How long we been in here?"

"You ain't gettin' nothin' out of me," the deputy said.

"Lovely," the sodden Amos commented softly. "Just lovely."

Slocum ignored him.

"Listen here, deputy," he said, "I don't know what's happened here so far, but I got a good idea of what's comin', and its comin' quick. If you got half a brain under that hat of yours, you'll let us out, and in a big hurry. We're here to help you."

Still, the deputy had no comment. In fact, he turned his head away.

"Jesus," Slocum swore under his breath. "Look, me and Amos here—"

"Are federal marshals," Amos piped up.

Slocum had clean forgotten all about that part, although he was past surprised the Amos had said marshals instead of Secret Service. Well, whatever game Amos was playing, Slocum would play along. He began to slap at his own pockets.

Sure enough, just as they'd missed his knife, they'd failed to take his wallet, and he still had that stupid badge Amos had pressed on him.

It was supposed to be used only in case of dire emergency, but Slocum figured this was as close as he was likely to get. He didn't much relish the idea of being stuck in a jail cell when and if the Carthage boys pulled in. One look at his face, and it would be all over.

Well, not that quick, he thought. They'd probably draw it out as long as possible.

Amos still had his badge, too, and he was already holding it out. It was apparent that he'd considered the same possibilities that Slocum just had.

"Look here, deputy," Amos said, holding his wallet forward, through the bars. "If you'd done a better job of checking us over for weapons, you might have come across this."

But the deputy never looked over at him, or at his badge. He simply said, "Shut up. You ain't gonna fool me, no sir," and walked out of the office, slamming the door behind him.

"Idiotic fool," Amos muttered, putting the badge back in his pocket. To Slocum he said, "Did they leave anything on you?"

"A boot knife," Slocum said, reaching down for it. "You give me enough time, I think the tip of it's narrow enough that I can pick this lock."

Amos shook his head. "Don't bother," he said, pulling a small leather case from his hip pocket. "They left me my lock-picking kit."

He unsnapped the cover, removed two small tools, and went to work on the door. "We are in the hands of a certified lunatic, you realize," he said as he worked. The tools made a tiny *click click* sound.

"Hope the citizens are a tad smarter," Slocum muttered.

Amos snorted. "I doubt it." The cell door swung open, and he put the tools back in their little case. "Nonetheless, they need saving. And so, if you haven't noticed, do we."

"Amos," Slocum whispered, keeping one eye on the door while he led the way from the cell and toward the gun rack where he saw his Colts hanging, "you're so dad blasted . . . British."

"You cut me to the very quick, Slocum, to the very quick."

Blue was just making his way up from the livery, and quietly noting the lack of activity—any activity—in the town, when Frank came barreling down the street toward him at a rolling trot.

"Sheriff Parker! Blue!" he called theatrically. It seemed poor old Frank lived half his life being out of breath. He was huffing and puffing already, and if he'd come from the office, he hadn't even been hurrying a block and a half.

"Easy, there, Frank!" Blue said, walking to meet him. "Slow down and calm yourself, for Christ's sake!"

"Did you get the other one?" Frank asked, all in a breathless rush as he skidded to a halt. "I brought in the other two, all by my lonesome!"

Frank bent over and grabbed his knees while he caught his breath. "Well, Gus, over at the saloon, he helped," Frank went on at last. "Buffaloed the both of 'em, but good! Oh, they're strappin' killers, they are! Mean-lookin', and they was armed to the teeth! I tell you, Blue, they—"

"Whoa, whoa, whoa!" Blue said, his voice raised in both anger and perplexity. "What other one? And what two? What in ever-lovin' tarnation you talkin' about, Frank?"

Frank rolled his eyes. "The killers!" he shouted impatiently. "I got two of Tom Crisp's killers locked up in our jail right this very minute! Ain't you been listenin' to a word I said?"

Blue took a breath. "Frank, I . . . oh, never mind," he said, and started for the jail. Frank probably had a couple of plain old saddle bums sitting in that old cell, cooling their heels and thinking nasty thoughts about what they were going to do to Frank—and him—once they got out.

Actually, Blue had just about decided that whoever shot poor old Tom Crisp was long gone, vanished off into the east.

"Well, I suppose we'd best see what you caught," Blue said, resigned to the situation. "They have red hair?"

"Huh?"

"Remember you told me that Arvil said the boys that shot Tom Crisp all had red hair?"

Frank frowned. "Well, they could'a been wearin' wigs. You know, disguised, like," he offered.

Annoyed, Blue grabbed Frank's shoulder and tugged him up the street. When they entered the jail, though, they were in for a surprise.

The cell was empty.

"I swear, Blue!" Frank began frantically. "I swear to Jesus they was in here! Ask the fellers what helped me drag 'em over from the saloon and lock 'em up, if you don't believe me!"

From behind the door, a voice spoke.

"Oh, I'd believe him if I was you, Blue."

Blue stiffened, and then he realized the voice sounded a tad familiar. No, very familiar. In fact, it made him feel awfully relieved.

He turned to the side and said, "Well, I'll be a straw-walkin' muskrat. Slocum? Is that you?"

And then the man, the one and only Slocum himself, stepped from behind the door, followed by a tall, yellow-headed fellow.

Blue barely noticed him, though. He set in to

pounding Slocum's shoulder and back, and saying things like, "By God!" and "You old sonofabitch!" and "I'll be double dogged!"

He barely noticed as poor Frank dejectedly slouched over to a chair and sat down, hard.

7

Rance, Rafe and Rufus Carthage slowly rode down toward town.

Rufus had been all for barreling in, whooping and hollering like they'd done those times before. It got the people all stirred up and scared shitless, and he liked that.

But Rance, the muscle-bound one of the bunch, had prevailed.

Young Rufus could tell that Rafe was disappointed, too. His dark, Mexican eyes were narrowed and just a tad downcast, and he looked up through bushy brows when he looked up at all. But despite that, Rafe hadn't said anything in protest, so Rufus kept his mouth shut, as well.

They proceeded at a plod until they got to the very edge of Hoopskirt, and stopped beside the millenary shop. It was a small, freestanding building, and it was dark, as were most of the buildings in town.

It was actually a little eerie, Rufus thought.

"Check in back," Rance said, and without a word,

Rafe and Rufus swung down off their mounts and walked around the building.

Eerie or not, Rufus knew there were people here to use and abuse. Woman, especially.

Rufus was tense and excited, so excited he could have lifted right out of his boots. He knew Rance figured there might be a woman living in the back of her shop, a lone woman.

And Rufus was in the mood for a lone woman, all right. He didn't care if she was fat or old or too tall or ugly. Hell, he didn't even care if she was a darkie. He just wanted a women, and any kind he could rustle up in hurry would do.

But when he and his brother reached the back of the building, Rafe snorted softly. "Ain't nobody here. The bitch musta gone home! What kind of a loony thing is that, goin' home when you got a perfectly good business to live in? Must be some kinda fancy-assed bitch to do that."

"Yeah," Rufus said in disgust. "No foolin'."

Angrily, he kicked at a clod of dirt in sheer frustration. He found himself wanting that "fancy-assed bitch" more and more. Hell, he didn't care if she was ninety years old and had a goiter the size of Nebraska!

"C'mon," Rafe muttered.

Rufus pulled himself away from his thoughts and followed Rafe back around the building.

"Nothin' there," Rufus reported to Rance while

he and Rafe got back up on their horses. "She must'a gone home after she closed up for the day."

"Goddamn fancy bitch," Rafe repeated with a scowl. He gathered his reins and grumbled, "Thinks a lot of herself, I bet. Thinks she's too damn grand to live in the back'a her shop, just cause she makes them stupid hats."

Then he got back down off his horse, picked up a stone from the ground, and hurled it though the big display window. It made a satisfying crash, and right away, Rufus saw a couple of heads pop out of buildings farther down the street, then pop back in, like tortoises into their shells.

"Goddamn feathery, glittery things," Rafe muttered, next to him.

Still looking at the town, Rufus scratched at the back of his head, pushing his sweat-stained hat forward in the process. "Somebody tell 'em we was comin' or somethin'?"

"Heard that before," Rance said, like he was bored. "Rafe, mount up."

Rafe did, wordlessly, although he had a grin on that dark face. *Rafe always was one for bustin' things up and likin' it,* Rufus thought with a smile.

Rufus liked it, too.

They rode south, three abreast down the center of the street, and into town.

• • •

"That's the story," Slocum said.

"In full," Amos added with a nod.

"Christ almighty," Blue muttered. "I hope to Christmas that you boys ain't right."

"So do we," Slocum said. "But I'm not countin' on it."

Amos hadn't felt the need to mention their badges again or their unofficial status, and Slocum hadn't said a word. He figured—like Amos must have done—that now they had the law on their side, and had no need to produce them. And that dumb deputy? He didn't seem to remember they'd ever said a thing, and Slocum wasn't about to remind him.

He was awfully glad to find that Hoopskirt's law was in the person of Bobbie Blue Parker. Why, he'd never thought to see him again, let alone be swept up in this mess in his company! Blue was a good man.

"And I'll bet my buggy—if I had it here, that is— that we're not wrong," Amos said. "Slocum is seldom incorrect about these things."

"I remember," Blue said.

Slocum grunted and gave a nod in Blue's direction.

"Well, what'll we do now?" asked the deputy, who had been sitting in a corner. Slocum had almost forgotten he was there.

"Oh. 'Scuse me, gents," said Blue, and swept out his hand. "Forgot to introduce you, formal-like, to my deputy. You took one another's names yet?"

"Haven't had the, um, pleasure," Amos said.

"Frank, John Slocum and Amos . . . sorry, didn't catch the last name."

"Marple," Amos said. He stood up and stuck out his hand. "Amos Piedmont Marple. Pleased to meet you. I think."

Piedmont? Slocum thought.

Frank stood up, too, and sheepishly took it. "Sorry, Amos." He turned. "You, too, Mr. Slocum. I'm right sorry for the mistake. If I'd'a knowed you was a friend'a Blue's . . ."

He trailed off into nothing.

Slocum neither stood up nor shook Frank's hand. It'd have to be a spell longer before he shook hands with the man who'd just about got them all killed. Not to mention had him buffaloed upside the head, and hard, too. His goddamn noggin *still* hurt.

Jackass.

Slocum got down to business. He said, "All right, Blue. First thing we got to do is get this town locked up and buttoned down, but it looks like you already done a pretty good job of that."

Blue said, "That was Frank's doin'."

"Good job, old boy," Amos said amiably.

But Slocum wasn't ready for forgive old Frank, and ignored both him and Amos. Instead, he went on, "The next thing we got to do is get some guards posted on every way into town. Blue, can you round up a few men? Trustworthy ones?"

Blue nodded. "Yup. I can get Neil and Ed from down at the saloon for starters. Neil's always there. How 'bout Ed, Frank?"

"He's there, Blue. Was when I brung these two in, anyhow," Frank piped up, then colored hotly. "Well, you know what I mean."

Slocum finally stood up. "Two men'll be enough for now. Let's get moving."

But before he could take a single, solitary step toward the door, the Carthage boys burst through it.

Except that, in what Slocum supposed was their gleeful anticipation, they tried to squeeze through the portal all at one time.

Amos, Blue and Slocum drew and fired in unison, just as Rance, the over-muscled, eldest brother, pushed his siblings to the side and rear, freeing his gun arm.

It wasn't in time, though.

Amos's slug took Rance in the right shoulder, Blue's hit him in the side, but Slocum's took him through the chest.

Rance looked surprised, that was all, and dropped to his knees. But before he died, he managed to fire his gun. His shot, probably fired blind, Slocum figured, missed both him and Amos—and winged Deputy Frank.

To Frank's holler of surprise and pain, Blue,

Amos and Slocum scattered and dropped to the floor, fully expecting the onslaught to begin.

But it didn't.

From outside, they heard the other two Carthage boys' boots scrambling, and then their horses racing off into the distance. They left their oldest brother in a pool of blood just inside the jailhouse door.

Slowly, Slocum got up and holstered his gun. Amos and Blue followed suit.

"I take it that was the Carthage brothers?" Blue asked, his tone droll.

"In the flesh," Amos said, kicked Rance's gun away, then gave the body a second kick, just to make certain he was doornail dead.

Frank, eyeing the prone body and clutching at his bleeding forearm, meekly inquired, "Is he . . . is he gone?"

They all ignored him.

Blue took down a rifle from the rack—and a sawed-off shotgun, as well—and grabbed several boxes of cartridges. "Help yourselves, boys," he said to Amos and Slocum.

"We're set," Slocum replied, and hauled Frank up to his feet like a rag doll. "You got a doctor in this burg?" he asked curtly.

"Y-yeah, Doc Whittle," Frank replied. He appeared to be glad to be addressed by Slocum in any way, shape or form. "He's got a place up over the—"

"Go see him," Slocum broke in.

"Then get somebody to clean up this mess," Blue said, pointing to Rance's body, which Amos was just stepping over.

Blue paused, then added, "And keep a lid on the town, Frank. I'm countin' on you. Tom Crisp's boys are gonna come ridin' in first thing in the morning. They can spell you."

Frank brightened, not that Slocum cared much, because he was already following Amos into the street at a dog trot. Blue brought up the rear, laden with cartridge boxes.

They hurried to the livery stable to get their horses. They had no time to waste.

"But what about Rance?" Rufus wailed as he and Rafe galloped north, over the plain. "We just . . . just left him there!"

"He was dead," Rafe shouted in reply. "Did you wanna get dead, too?"

"But we just lit out! Seems like we should'a done somethin', if only shoot those goddamn bastards what killed him!"

Rafe pulled up his horse at last, and Rufus did, too.

"That's right, Rufus, you dumb little shit, we just lit out," Rafe said, his dark eyes narrowed. "They was waitin' for us. Waitin' for us! Sonofabitch! Don't that Slocum never go away?"

Rufus perked up his ears. He hadn't got in close enough to see much of anything before Rance shoved him and Rafe out of the way. "It was Slocum? The one what put us in Yuma? That Slocum?"

"Yeah," Rafe spat, "that one. Jesus Christ, Rufus. I mean, how many Slocums can there be? And that sonofabitchin' limey, Amos Marple, was in there with him, too!"

"But how'd they know we was comin'?" Rufus asked, bewildered. "Where'd they come from, anyway? I mean, how'd they know we was comin' to Hoopskirt, let alone exactly *there*?"

"I don't know, goddammit," Rafe said, gathering his reins again. "What do I look like, a blasted fortune teller? Now just ride, will you?"

He lashed Rufus's bay across the rump, and Rufus lurched forward. Rufus didn't know where they were going and he was half-afraid to ask. Wherever it was, it was in a great big hurry.

He rode blindly, following Rafe's lead.

8

"Goddamn them Carthage boys," Blue swore angrily beneath his breath as he quickly saddled his roan.

"Did you say something?" Amos asked him. He, too was slinging tack over his bay and tying off latigo like a man possessed.

"I said that them Carthages sure picked a swell time to come bangin' into town." Blue bridled his horse, and buckled the throat latch. "Iffen they'd rode in anywhere close to daylight, we'd have had 'em, just like that." He snapped his fingers.

Amos knew he was right. He'd checked the skies while they'd hurried down to the livery, and he figured they had perhaps an hour and a half before the clouds moved in to cover the moon. But for the moment, it would be reasonably clear—if dangerous—going. The moon was at less than half full, but high.

Slocum apparently agreed with him. He hadn't said a word, but Amos had caught him looking skyward while they were still outside, rushing down the street. And they were about to be outside again, because Slocum was leading that absurd-looking Appaloosa from its stall.

Amos has seen a lot of horses in his time, but never one that looked like that.

Leave it to Slocum!

Amos led his bay outside, followed by Blue and his strawberry roan. As one, the three men mounted.

Also as one, without a word, they broke into a trot, then pushed it to an easy canter. They headed north.

Amos let Slocum take the lead, and he noticed that Blue did too, without any argument. Blue must know that Slocum was the best tracker west of the Mississippi—probably east of it, too—and once again, Amos wondered just where and when the two had known each other. It must have been in a time of trouble, though, for the two worked together seamlessly.

Almost as well as he and Slocum worked together, Amos thought, a tad chagrined.

After a few minutes, and once the town was out of sight, Slocum reined his horse down to a walk, then a stop, and then cut off the road. "This way," he said. And they followed.

They followed him at a jog or a walk, and every once in a while, at dead run.

And then they hit rock.

"Goddammit," Blue cursed, pushing his hat back nearly to the hairline. "We ain't gonnna find a thing.

These low hills are solid rock. Volcanic. Won't take a print no matter what."

"We've lost them, then," Amos said dejectedly. Wonderful. Now they'd have to start all over again, and the Lord only knew how many lives would be lost during the delay.

But Slocum didn't speak. Instead, he sat his mount and thoughtfully reached for his fixings pouch and proceeded to roll himself a quirlie.

As Slocum struck a lucifer and held its flame to the tip of his smoke, Blue said, "Well, Slocum? What're we gonna do now?"

Slocum shook out his match.

"He's thinking," whispered Amos. He'd seen this behavior before.

"Well, he's gonna think his way right into dead dark," Blue hissed back, and pointed up. Sure enough, the cloud bank, once off in the distance, had moved closer. It would cover the moon entirely in a few minutes. And the clouds held something worse: flashes of distant lightning.

There was no thunder yet, and Amos remembered that in Arizona, thunder and lightning didn't always mean rain.

Sometimes it meant nothing, sometimes it meant hail—like the other night—and sometimes it meant wind so fierce that it snapped sapling tree trunks in half and literally drove people mad with its howl, battering sand and pelting twigs and cactus.

He surely didn't wish to be caught out in one of those. Years ago, he'd weathered one in a rickety lean-to with Slocum and a Apache squaw. It didn't seem to bother Slocum any—or the Indian woman, for that matter—but it had scared him to death.

He'd felt as if any moment, the angry wind would swirl up that lean-to and send him straight home to heaven.

Slocum reined his horse around to face them. He said, "Been thinking what I'd do if I was Rufus and Rafe Carthage. And I can only come up with one thing. I'd go back to town."

"Huh?" said Blue. "Why the hell would they do somethin' stupid like that?"

"Because they've got to figure that most of the men—most of the best men, anyhow—are already chasin' them down, or on their way to it," Slocum said, and exhaled a plume of smoke. "Which leaves the old, the useless and all the women in town. Sides, they got a mighty big bone to pick with Hoopskirt in general—and us in particular—over their brother." He shrugged. "Leastwise, it's what I'd do if I was Rafe and Rufus."

Amos suddenly perked up. "That's why they veered off their path and came up into these rocks, isn't it?"

"My guess," replied Slocum.

"Well, what are we doin' sitting out here?" Blue demanded. "Let's get back to town! If you can backtrack us back to the road, Slocum, I could find my way to Hoopskirt from there blindfolded."

Frank had done a good job of marshaling the menfolk, Lucy thought.

This surprised her. Usually Frank was as useless as tits on a boar hog, but he sort of seemed to be in his element, giving orders and bossing people around. Of course, he didn't have any orders for her or the other girls.

Naturally.

It just slayed her how he could send old Phineas Coit down to the end of the street with that old shotgun of his to "keep watch." Hell, Phineas couldn't see much farther than the end of his nose, and God knows he couldn't hit the side of a barn with a handful of beans.

Now, she, on the other hand, had been raised up in Kansas, in Pawnee country, and had cut her teeth on a rifle stock. More than once, she'd taken aim and shot an attacking Pawnee warrior dead off his pony, at more than fifty paces. And that was when she was just a kid of ten or twelve.

But no, Frank had her back behind the bar, brewing coffee and making sandwiches. Right at the moment, she was standing on the trap door to the cellar, where they stored beer kegs. In the winter, it actually kept them cool. Well, cooler than they were now.

They also kept their root vegetables down there, and their big pickle jars, full of cukes and eggs mostly, for those rare occasions when Barney, who owned the place, completely lost his mind and offered free food with the drinks.

Which wasn't very often. Lucy would have laid money on there being five-year-old carrots down there. Not that she was about to look, mind you. She'd never been down there, but one time Barney came up the steps, carrying a beer keg, with a great big old black widow hitching a ride on his sleeve.

To say that she didn't much care for spiders was like saying that Marie Antoinette didn't much care for guillotines.

Lucy moved back down to the other end of the bar, taking with her the meat she'd just sliced. There, with one eye on the old pot-bellied stove and the two pots of perking coffee atop it, she cut bread into thick slices and slathered it with butter, slapped on some roast beef or roast chicken, the topped it with a second slice of buttered bread.

She did this with a certain amount of gusto. Each slap of meat was a slap to the face of Frank, for thinking women were so useless in general, and that she was, in particular.

He'd sent the other girls upstairs, supposedly to lock themselves in their rooms.

As if their rooms had locks!

Where did Frank think he was? A girls' boarding school?

This brought an unbidden smile to her lips. "Mr. Barney Hansens's School for Young Ladies of Good Breeding."

Ha! Well, they were all good breeders—good at the practicing of it, anyhow.

She thought that maybe, after she got these damned sandwiches made, she'd go upstairs and get Josie and Annie. If she could sneak past Frank, that was.

If those animals who killed Tom Crisp came back, they wouldn't be safe up there. Why, it was like hanging out a welcome sign!

Frank had a good heart, she supposed, but he could be goddamn dumb sometimes.

All right, most of the time.

She finished the last sandwich and put it on the heaping plate—*that should keep the sentries fed for a while*, she thought—then started down the bar and toward the stair.

Frank looked up from his stupor. "Where you think you're goin', Lucy?" he demanded.

"Upstairs," she said. "I'm gonna get the girls. To, uh, help me."

"You leave them girls be," Frank said, glancing up from the short list of "recruits" he'd drummed up for sentry duty. Oh, he was "Mr. In-Charge" tonight, blast his hide.

"I want 'em hid out," he said officiously. "Just in case. And bring me one'a them sandwiches."

Lucy signed. "Chicken or beef?"

Frank considered for a moment. "Both," he said at last. "And a cup'a coffee. Black, with three spoons'a sugar."

Using all the sarcasm she had in her, which was quite a bit, she said, "Oh, yes sir, deputy, right away, deputy, sir."

And it was all lost on Frank. He said, "That's more like it," and went back to his little map of the town, and telling poor little Lloyd Dobbins, who was shaking like a proverbial leaf, where to stand guard. Hell, Lloyd was only fifteen!

A murder of crows, she thought, *a gaggle of geese, a herd of cattle . . . I wonder what they call a whole mess of idiots?*

Well, if these Carthage boys—or Carter boys, Frank wasn't too sure—came calling, she was ready for them. She had no pistol, but deep in her apron pocket, she had a shiny butcher knife.

And Lord knows, she knew how to use it.

Just let them try anything funny with me! she thought, and poured Frank his goddamn coffee.

Rufus and Rafe, had, in fact, taken the path of least resistance.

Or more resistance, depending on how you looked at it.

They had indeed sought out the patch of rocky ground, of which there were quite a few surrounding the town of Hoopskirt. In fact, this surface stone ringed the town, broken only in patches. It was how Hoopskirt had gotten its name.

But the symmetry of this notion was lost upon the brothers. They were at the west side of town, looking down on the lone, balding, aging man standing guard on a side street.

"He ain't got nothin' but an old flintlock!" sneered Rufus, who had the better eyesight of the two.

"Hold your pecker, Rufus," Rafe said curtly. "Don't you feel that wind comin' up?"

"Well, yeah," Rufus said. He had, in fact, raised his collar against it some time ago. "So?"

"We're in for a real rip-snorter," Rafe continued. "And what happens when there's a real rip-snorter startin' up?"

"People go inside," replied Rufus, then added, "I get you. You figure once the wind picks up enough, everybody's gonna desert their posts, right?"

Rafe nodded.

Already the sky was darkening quite a bit, and Rufus could hardly make his brother out in the gloom. When he stared back down toward the town and the sentry, he could barely see the first, and couldn't see the second at all.

"I get you, brother," Rufus said, and swung down off his horse.

"What you doin' that for?" Rafe demanded.

"Ain't gonna ride this nag over ground I ain't gonna be able to seen in a minute. Gonna lead him. Then show me the way to the whorehouse!"

"You got a one-track mind," Rafe said. He dismounted, too. "You forgot all about Rance?"

Rufus was a little ashamed, and said, "No, I ain't forgot him, Rafe. But you're the one who pointed out that he's past carin' whether I mourn him with my hat off and in a black suit, or whether he's mourned betwixt the legs of a whore." He paused for a moment. "Knowin' Rance, he'd probably like it better if I did it with the whore. Mayhap several."

"You think too much," Rafe said. "Makes my head hurt sometimes.

"But I reckon you're right, boy," he went on. "I mean, that I was right in the goddamn first place. I'm gonna take a piece outta that town, though. Gonna do it for Rance."

Rufus nodded. "And I'll help you. As soon as I get me a couple whores out of my system."

The wind rose to a low hum, then the beginnings of a shriek. The sky, already dark, was now eerily yellowed by blowing dust and grit.

And at last, the brothers, bandannas tied over their noses and mouths against the wind, started leading their horses down toward Hoopskirt.

9

Slocum, Amos and Blue were back on the road again, and just in time.

The wind had risen to the point where a man couldn't see the rump of the horse in front of him. Slocum had turned over his reins to Blue, who was in the lead, and Amos had given his reins to Slocum. It was the blind leading the blind as they slowly made their way back toward Hoopskirt.

They couldn't talk. Even if the howling wind would have allowed them to be heard, they probably would have choked on a mouthful of sand and grit at the first parting of their lips.

Slocum had pulled his bandanna up over his nose and mouth. It helped some. He couldn't see if Blue or Amos had thought to do the same.

And he found himself envying Blue those damned tinted glasses of his. They might make things darker, but they'd surely keep the grit out of a fellow's eyes.

And he was counting on those eyes.

And then he realized he didn't remember whether Blue had even worn those glasses. Probably not, dammit. It was dark when they'd started out, and he hadn't noticed. He'd been too keen on galloping out hell bent for leather, too keen on finding the quarry.

That'll teach me to pay attention to details, he thought grimly.

It began to rain; scattered at first, then big, pelting drops that were blowing in at an angle, almost sideways, and hurt and stung where they hit uncovered skin.

"Great, just great," muttered Slocum beneath the roar of the storm, beneath the thunder that now came crashing and seemed to roll on forever.

Slowly, they trudged on.

Hopefully, toward Hoopskirt.

The old man with the long gun had disappeared from the alley's mouth by the time the Carthage boys made their way down into town.

They took shelter from the wind and the rain in the alley, and Rufus mopped at his sodden brow with his equally sodden sleeve. "Holy cripes!" he shouted. "When it rains, it don't josh around!"

"What?" hollered Rafe, leaning closer.

Rufus shook his head, indicating never mind, and leaned back against the side of the nearest building. If he was ever in the mood for a beer and a woman and a soft bed, this was it. And then, of course, a little ripping things up.

He'd rest first, though.

It came to him that a man forgot about things like being out in a bad storm when he was surrounded, day and night, by thick adobe walls and prison guards.

Rafe started up the alley, still leading his mount, and Rufus followed. They hitched their horses to a rail that was somewhat out of the wind and left them standing there, heads down, tails tucked.

Squinting against the blow, Rafe shouted in Rufus's ear, "I think the saloon's up this way!"

Rufus nodded eagerly. It was the best news he'd heard in a coon's age.

Moving from window to doorway, hanging on to each ensuing handhold for dear life, they moved up the main street.

Lucy was just carrying a tray of sandwiches and coffee and beer out to Frank and the men who'd come in from the storm. But then, from the corner of her eye, she saw two dark figures moving across the gaily painted front window, toward the batwing doors.

Now, Lucy knew every man, woman and child in Hoopskirt, and she could recognize most of them from two blocks away.

These figures, she didn't recognize.

She didn't take the time to think about it. She simply ducked down beneath the level of the bartop, and crept down to the far end, to the trap door to the beer cellar.

She raised it and went down into the darkness, tray and all, and then softly lowered the door after her. She was searching for a candle, a lantern, anything, when she heard, from above, the sound of chairs scraping back and toppling.

She froze.

"That's him," said a voice she didn't know. "That's one'a the fellers what was in the jail when Rance got shot."

She heard Frank's voice, so thin and pathetic it was almost unrecognizable, saying, "No, no, you're wrong! I never—"

A gunshot rang out, followed directly by a heavy thud, and Frank didn't speak again.

"Serves you right, law dog," spat another new voice. The second man. "What are all you boy's doin' in here? Hidin'?"

There were five other men up there, but she didn't hear a word out of any of them. They were either cowards or very wise men.

She suspected it was some of both.

"Put your weapons on that table then back away from it," said the first voice. "All of em'. C'mon, move it!"

There were a few thuds of metal on wood, and then the voice said, "All right. Over to that table. There. By the window, where I can see you. Sit down. All except you," continued the first voice. "Get back behind the bar and rustle us up a couple'a beers. In fact, let's all have us a beer, in fond memory of our late brother, Rance, that got himself killed by this stinkin' deputy and his buddies."

Boots thudded overhead toward the table at the front window. And Lucy thought, *Clever bastards, they're using them as a screen, too, so nobody'll take a chance on shooting them from outside.*

Another pair of footsteps neared, crossed overhead, then went down the bar, to the kegs.

"Hey, what kind of sandwiches is them?" the voice asked again.

She heard Otis Hopkins stutter out, "Ch-chicken and b-beef, s-sir."

"Well, go get 'em. The whole platter. My brother and me, we had us a long ride, and we're hungry enough to eat a horse."

Lucy gulped. She had half the remaining sandwiches on the plate she'd been carrying to the table. She hoped some wiseacre wouldn't remark on it.

"Where's your women?" said one of the voices. "I feel the need for female company, if you know what I mean."

The little "joke" raised no laughter. There was only silence. Well, God bless them for that, anyway.

"I said," the voice repeated, this time in anger, "where do y'all keep your women? Your whores! They hidin' or somethin'?"

Still, there was not a word. Lucy closed her eyes and began to pray for the girls upstairs. She knew what men like these did with women. It wasn't pleasant, and it wasn't pretty.

There was a long silence, and then another shot that caused her to jump and nearly spill the tray. She caught it just as she heard another body drop to the floor.

"All right," he demanded. "Who's gonna be next?"

"You shot Otis!" someone called. She thought it was Irv Staples, who ran the general store. "What'd you do that for, you coward?"

Another shot. Another body, presumably Irv's, who had never hurt so much as a fly, thudded on the planks somewhere above her.

The deeper of the stranger's voices mumbled, "Good eats, Rufus. You oughta try one. Beer's not bad, either."

"In a damn minute, Rafe," said Rufus, who had a name at last. "I got business to attend to first. And it looks like I ain't gonna get nothin' from these stupid-ass shit heels."

Lucy realized she was crying, silently.

Rufus shouted, "Hey, gals! You'd best come down, or me and my brother are gonna start pepperin' the ceiling with bullets. You can either come down and have a sandwich with a feller, or you can get shot up. Your choice."

Lucy couldn't hear the doors slowly creaking open, but she knew they were, because Rufus shouted, "Now, that's more like it, ladies! Come on down! Don't be shy!"

Oh, how Lucy wished she had a gun, any gun! There'd be no one behind the bar. If she had a pistol or a rifle, she could simply sneak up the stair again, pop up from behind the bar, and shoot both those vermin before they knew she was there. It would be a whole lot easier than shooting a Pawnee off his pony.

After all, they had just murdered three men upstairs, and they had undoubtedly killed old Tom Crisp this afternoon.

No jury would convict her. They might even award her a medal.

But Barney, wherever he was at the moment, didn't keep any firearms down here. At least, not that she knew of. If she could only find some kind of light . . .

Upstairs, Rufus was saying, "Josie. That's a purty name. C'mere, Josie."

Lucy carefully set the tray of drinks and food on the floor, shoved it quietly back under the narrow stair where she wouldn't accidently step on it and give herself away, and began feeling for matches.

"That's right, Josie, honey. Now, take off your clothes."

Lucy stopped with a jolt and craned her head up.

Surely she couldn't have heard him correctly!

The sound of the wind had died down enough that she heard the cock of his pistol. "Take 'em off, Josie. Down to the skin. And then come on over here and sit on my lap."

"You, too, blondie," said Rafe. He had to be talking to Annie Hanna. She was the only blonde in the place besides Lucy. "And be quick about it. I wanna see them titties a'yourn. I wanna see 'em right in my face, if you know what I mean."

Tears streaming down her cheeks, Lucy began again to feel and fumble for a match. She felt the sticky, sick, unmistakable web of a black widow brush her ankle, and heard it rip.

She fought off the nausea rising in her throat, and covered her mouth briefly. And once the feeling had passed and she was certain nothing was crawling on her, she kept feeling along dusty shelves for a match and a candle, or most of all, a firearm.

There had to be a gun. There just had to be.

10

Thankfully, the wind seemed to be lessening, and the rain was actually falling on them now, not coming from the side in heavy, wind-whipped sheets.

Blue, Amos and Slocum picked up the pace. Slocum had to admit—to himself, anyhow—that he hadn't appreciated being led around like a kid on a pony. But whatever worked, worked.

They were still on the road, riding through a slop of clay and gravel at a jog now, and each under his own power.

Blue glanced skyward. "We're gonna beat 'em back to town," he said, over the steadily decreasing sound of the storm. Weather, at least violent weather, passed quickly out here sometimes. Fortunately, this had been one of them.

"Wouldn't bet on it," Slocum said. "I wouldn't bet on anything for certain with those boys." He pushed his Appy into a slow lope to take the lead.

Blue and Amos were right behind him.

They increased their speed as the weather permitted, and by the time they reach Hoopskirt, the rainfall was light, but steady, and the wind had ceased to blow. The worst of the storm had moved on, toward the northeast.

They headed toward the livery, but halfway there, Amos reined up. "Dear God," he whispered.

Slocum and Blue followed his gaze toward the saloon. Two men, heads turned with an expression that could only be shame, sat at a table in the front window.

Bodies littered the floor, and Blue whispered, "Dear God. Not Frank."

Behind the men at the table, Rufus Carthage was holding a gun on a stark naked woman. Her face was swollen, not only with tears, but with bruises just beginning to show. He had her on her back across a table, his britches down were around his ankles, and he was screwing her with a vengeance.

His brother, Rafe, was engaged in much the same activity, except his victim was bent over, hanging onto the bar for dear life, and he was taking her from the backside. His gun was not pointed at her, but at the men at the table.

Not that they needed to be covered. The men at the table looked far too scared and ashamed to move.

"Aw, shit," cursed Blue beneath his breath. "They got Josie and little Annie."

Amos was already off his bay and tossing his reins over the rail. "I'll take the back," he said, without humor. He was all business.

"We'll take the front doors," Slocum replied as he and Blue dismounted at the same time.

Amos trotted down an alley and disappeared. Slocum and Blue secured their mounts, then Slocum signaled to Blue to take the nearest side of the bar.

Slocum, himself, took off across the street, keeping to the shadows, in order to bypass the saloon and then come up from the opposite side.

He slipped and slid on the clay mud, but he didn't fall, wouldn't let himself fall, by God. This was too important for anybody to mess it up now.

At last, he worked his way back up to the saloon. Blue was already on the far side, and a whippoorwill's call from his left, back in the alley, told him that Amos was in position.

Good old Amos!

He drew his gun, then nodded at Blue.

They began, slowly, to work their way up toward the windows.

Rufus had finished with his girl, and shoved her roughly off the table. She landed on the floor in a fetal position. He set down his gun in order to hoist his britches up again.

Without checking Rafe or Blue or anybody else, Slocum fired through the glass.

Things began to happen awfully fast. Rufus, damn his hide, was only hit in the shoulder, and grabbed his gun off the table before he went all the way down to the floor.

In his fervor to get that horse-murdering Rufus,
Slocum had ignored Rafe, who jumped over the bar
just as Blue's shot rang out. Slocum heard him yelp,
but he wasn't hurt bad enough to keep him from
returning fire.

The men at the front table scrambled down and
under it, pulling their chairs down and around them
like the walls of a fort, just as Slocum jumped back
to avoid flying glass from Rufus's returned fire.

During a brief lull, Slocum heard Blue mutter,
"Well, shit."

Slocum knew just how he felt.

He should have waited. Should have checked the
whole scene before he let his pent-up anger and rage
get to him. He would have kicked himself, but there
was no time.

Rufus was firing again.

Blue ducked down and back to avoid both the
slugs and the shattering glass, while Slocum took
advantage of the confusion to take another shot at
Rufus.

But Rufus had pulled over the table on which he
had just taken the girl, and wouldn't stick his goddamn head out. And Slocum had to be careful not
to hit the girl as she crawled across the floor, bawl-
ing, toward the naked blonde.

And to add insult to injury, he heard Rafe call
out, "Some kind of fun, right, kid?"

And Rufus, damn his hide, hollered back, "You

bet, Rafe. Only wish Rance could'a been here!" And then he laughed.

Laughed!

Well, Slocum would give him something to laugh about, all right.

Just then, the bar's back door burst open, and Amos came through it, guns blazing. He put a slug into Rufus—Slocum could tell, because he gave out with a girlish, high-pitched yelp—but Rafe put a slug into Amos. Amos grabbed at his side, got off one more shot, which went up and hit nothing but the ceiling, and fell against the wall.

He slid to the floor, leaving a long smear of blood in his wake.

"Rafe!" Rufus shouted. "Can you walk?"

"I can run, little brother," came the reply from behind the bar. "But first I'd like to finish off these assholes, if you don't mind!"

Younger brother or no, Rufus took over. "Tough," he said. "Get down to the end of the bar. I'll cover you while you go for the back door. We'll meet at the horses."

When Rafe made no sound, no scratch of boots against wood, Rufus shouted, *"Now!"*

Muttering something—probably vile—in Spanish, Rafe moved.

And he moved so fast that Rufus was firing a covering round of slugs before he knew what he was doing. When Rafe got out the back door, Rufus wasted no time, either. He grabbed the wrist of the weeping, scared, naked girl he'd just raped, twirled her around, and used her for a living shield as he backed toward the door.

Just as he thought, the fools stopped shooting. "Anything to save a cheap whore," he muttered as he reached the rear door.

He pushed her away as he let himself out and raced for the horses.

He had no mind for the pain in his shoulder. He'd found long ago that he was able to just turn off the pain when it was necessary. And this was one of those times. He'd seen Rafe take a slug in his side, but he wasn't too worried.

Why, Rafe had taken five bullets before Slocum and that goddamn limey brought them down the last time, and he'd lived to tell the tale!

Rafe was having trouble mounting up, though, and without a word, Rufus ran to him and boosted him up.

"Thanks," muttered Rafe as Rufus got on his own horse. "Smarts a might."

"Yeah," replied Rafe, as they lashed their horses out of town.

Slocum and Blue ran through the doors, guns still drawn. While Blue raced straight through, to the back door, Slocum knelt beside Amos.

The slug had taken him in the side, but so far as Slocum could figure, it hadn't hit anything vital. Still, he shouted, "Don't just sit there, get the doc!" to the fellows still cowering beneath the table.

Quickly, he took off his jacket and threw it to the little gal that Rufus had used for cover, but that was all he had to toss. Whimpering, she caught it, and he turned back to Amos.

"Amos!" he demanded. "Amos, you wake up! I mean it. Talk to me, man."

Amos's eyes fluttered, and his lips moved. Slocum bent closer to hear. "Stop shouting as if I were in the next county," Amos whispered. "I can hear you perfectly well, you lout."

Slocum broke out in a grin.

The back door opened, and Slocum automatically twisted toward it, gun leveled.

But it was only Blue. "Don't shoot," he said. "They're long gone. How's he doin'?" he asked, indicating Amos.

"I believe I shall live," Amos said, a bit louder. "Would someone please force brandy down my throat?"

Rather rudely, Slocum dropped him back down on the floor with a mutter of, "Goddamn shirker . . ."

To Blue, he asked, "Can we run 'em down tonight?"

"I'd say no," Blue replied. "The horses are all in, and besides—"

From behind the bar came the sound of a door creaking open and thudding back on its hinges. Footsteps rose up from somewhere below. The door banged shut again, and a tousled, blond, fairy-curled head of hair surrounding the face of an angel rose from behind the bar.

Slocum blinked.

The girl, who looked to be in her middle twenties, took one look around, saw the two naked girls, one cowering behind Slocum's jacket, and angrily said, "Dear God! Have you men no pity? Just 'cause a girl's gotta stoop low to make a livin' for herself don't mean she got no modesty or shame!"

She reached behind her to a hook on the wall and pulled down an apron. She wrapped it around the little blonde, got her to her feet, then scooped up the girl in Slocum's jacket.

"At least somebody's a gentleman," she snapped.

Sheltering the naked, shivering, weeping girls the best that she could, she soothed them and ferried them up the stairs.

"Who in the Sam Hill was that?" Slocum said, staring after her, gape-mouthed.

"Lucy Treadwell," answered Blue matter-of-factly. "She's second-in-command around the bar. Now, I figure all this wet clay we call ground is gonna hold their tracks pretty damned good, and when Tom Crisp's boys come in the morning, we can—"

"Where the hell was she during all . . . this?" Slocum asked.

She was out of sight now, but he still stared up, toward the empty landing around the corner where she'd disappeared.

"Hid in the cellar, probably. Now, like I was sayin' . . ." Blue continued. But he didn't get a chance to finish because they both paused and looked up at the thudding bootsteps coming up the walk.

"Doc Whittle's here," announced the lone man still sitting at the table. Slocum figured he was making mental notes to tell his grandkids. At his age, that was about all he could do.

The doctor, portly and carrying a black bag, burst in a half-second later. He took one look around the corpse-strewn floor and said, "Dear God in Heaven. What happened here? I mean, I heard the shots, but I never expected anything like this!"

"Long story," Slocum replied. "Best check the others first." With the assurance of one who has seen many, many wounds, most of them fatal, he pronounced, "Amos, here, is gonna make it fine."

"Thank you so very much for that diagnosis," Amos said snidely.

He was still rubbing his head from being dropped on the floor by Slocum. "Don't mind me. I'll just quietly bleed to death over here in the corner. Go on about your business."

Blue, who seemed to be paying Amos no attention whatsoever, asked, "You want me to answer your question or not, Slocum?"

"You already did," Slocum said. "Clay, tracks, horses are done in, we'll wait till morning when Crisp's boys ride in. Did I forget anything?"

Blue threw his hands in the air. "No, nothin'. Nothin' at all."

"This one's alive," announced the doctor. He was hunched over Frank's body. "Don't know for how much longer, though. You men, help me get him up on a table. No, the bar."

While Blue and Slocum carried Frank gently to the bar, the doctor went to Amos.

"You can wait," the doctor said curtly after taking a peek.

Slocum heard Amos's dry mutter of, "And thank you so very much for that bit of encouragement," and bit back a grin.

"Goddamn you, Frank," Blue grumbled as they lifted him up to the bar. "Didn't I teach you, the very first thing when I hired you, not to go and get yourself shot up?"

"He can't hear you," Doc Whittle said as he stood up and came over. He opened his bag. "Which is probably a very good thing."

"Why?" asked Blue.

"Because he won't scream and thrash while I try to get this bullet out. I hate it when they do that."

11

Once the operation was over with and the slug had been taken from a spot very near to poor Frank's lung and tossed unceremoniously into the spittoon, the doctor went to see to Amos.

"Nothing to it," Doc Whipple said. He has Amos stripped out of his shirt and sitting up in a chair. "Just hit the meat. Went all the way through, clean as a whistle."

"And into the wall," said Slocum. With his pocket knife, he worked at it, then popped something out into his hand. He tossed it over to Amos, who caught it, then grimaced at the movement. "Just in case you want a keepsake," Slocum said.

"You'd best take a look at those gals upstairs," Slocum added belatedly. "They had a pretty rough time of it."

"Shot?" asked the doctor.

"Nope, but scuffed up real damned good. The Carthage boys don't play nice, if you know what I mean."

The doctor sighed and picked up his bag again. "I do indeed. In all my life, I've never been called upon to see so many wounded people, nor sign so many death certificates, in one night. You see that Frank stays still, Blue."

Blue, who was standing by the bar at the still-unconscious Frank's head, nodded.

As the doctor trudged up the stairs, Amos shrugged back into his shirt over the copious swathing of bandages provided by the doctor and in a surprisingly cheery tone—probably due to a dose of laudanum the doc had forced on him—said, "Would there be such an animal as a hotel in this fair city?"

Blue shook his head. "Nope. But you're welcome to stay over at the jail."

Amos snorted. "Thank you, but I believe I've seen enough of the jail for one night."

"Stay at my place, then," Blue said. "I got a horsehair sofa. Don't know how comfortable it is, though. Ain't never been called on to sleep on it."

"High time it was broken in, then," Amos said. "What about Slocum?"

Slocum wasn't looking at him. He was staring up those stairs, at that empty landing the doc had just navigated.

"Don't worry about me," he said. "I'll find a roost."

Amos scraped his chair back. "You always do. Well, I'm going to get some sleep. Which way to your home, Blue?"

"Down the street a block, turn left, and it's the

first little adobe on your right," Blue replied. "Door's open. Make yourself to home."

"Thank you. Good night, Blue. Sometime we shall have to have a chat about your past with our old friend Slocum. Slocum?"

Slocum reluctantly pulled his gaze from those stairs. Damned if he couldn't keep his mind on anything but that Lucy gal! "What?" he said.

Amos was already beside the batwing doors. "I said . . . oh, never mind. See you in the morning, old bean."

"Right," said Slocum. "In the morning. And I may be a lot of things, but I ain't no bean."

"Hey, Slocum," Blue called teasingly, "hadn't you best go up and see how the doc's coming with them little gals?"

"Oh, shut up," Slocum replied, but he began to mount the stairs, anyway.

Lucy stood in the hallway, outside Josie's door, tapping her toe and waiting for word from the doctor. The door opened at last, and she caught a glimpse of Josie, tucked in like a five-year-old and sound asleep, before the doc closed the door behind him.

"She's banged up the worst of the two," he said quietly. "Almost got a broken nose, and she's gonna be a mass of bruises in the morning, but she'll be all right. I gave her something to help her sleep. She's more hysterical than anything else. You got anybody else for me to look at, or can I go on home, now?"

"No," said a deep voice from the landing. Lucy turned toward it. It was one of the strangers, the kind one who'd given his jacket to Josie. "That's it, Doc Whittle. Thanks."

"Same payment plan as usual, Doc?" Lucy called after him.

"Fine," the doctor answered in a mumble, although he didn't seem too happy about it.

Slocum brushed shoulders with the doc in the hallway and came to stand beside Lucy. To the sound of Doc's retreating footsteps on the stairs, she said, "Thank you. I should have said that before."

Slocum tipped his hat. He had a handsome head of dark hair. "We were lucky we got here when we did. Wish we could'a got here sooner, Lucy."

She arched a brow.

"One of the fellers downstairs told me your name," he explained. His cool, green eyes were like a breath of spring in this desert, where she'd spent her entire life. "Anything I can do to help?"

"Your name?" she asked.

His face, more rugged than handsome but still compellingly attractive, briefly took on a slight rosy shade, which she found endearing.

The blush faded, and he said, "Oh, sorry. It's Slocum, ma'am."

"You can tell me just what the devil is going on,

Mr. Slocum," she said. She moved across the hall and opened the door. "For instance, who you are, and who those beasts were tonight."

"Happy to, Lucy," he said, following her in. "And it's just Slocum." He took off his hat. "No 'mister' to it."

"All right, Slocum."

Somewhere, in that black, wet night, the two remaining Carthage brothers ran out of steam.

At least, Rufus did.

He was tired, his horse was tired, his arm ached him something terrible and he couldn't see where the hell they were going. He just reined in his horse and stopped.

A couple paces later Rafe must have realized he was alone, because he stopped and twisted around in his saddle.

"What?" Rafe said. "Why you stoppin'?"

Rufus figured that Rafe had to be as wet and grouchy as he was, which was quite a bit. So he managed to temper his tone—always a good idea around Rafe, anyhow—and said, "Rafe, I'm all in. We put a couple of hours between us and that town, and there ain't nobody chasin' us that I can tell of. I figured it was time we took us a little break, maybe got us some sleep, you know? Mayhap you could dig this slug outta my shoulder while we're all it."

Rafe just glared at him.

"I mean," Rufus continued, "these horses is all in, too. What we gonna do if they come chasin' after us tomorrow and we used up the horses tonight, stumblin' around out here in the dark?"

He waited while Rafe thought this over. You could almost see him thinking, the way it crawled across his face.

At last, Rafe twisted back around in his saddle and dismounted without a word, and Rufus let out a little sigh of relief.

It was bad enough, everything that had happened to them in the space of the last few hours. He didn't want Rafe turning on him, too.

They had come far enough from town that they had left the clay mud behind, and had been traveling over rock for some time. They hobbled the horses— there being no vegetation to tie them to—and sat on the ground without a boulder or rock to shelter them, and with nothing softer than their thin bedrolls over black rock to sit on.

Rafe got out his pocket knife, but didn't offer to start on Rufus. Instead, he began to dig at the slug that had winged him in the side.

"Wanna know what I think?" Rafe finally said, once he popped the bullet out. It couldn't have been buried too deep.

"What?" asked Rufus.

"I think Rance's still alive back there. I think they

got him locked up somewhere. I think maybe he's just waitin' for us to come get him."

Now, Rufus and Rafe had both seen Rance die. They'd both seen him hit three times, seen him fall with the blood pooling fast, both seen it as they turned and ran.

But part of Rafe must be thinking that his brawny elder brother, the one he could never best in a fight, the one who had always been in charge, couldn't possibly be dead.

Rufus knew how he felt. He'd been having those feelings, too.

But, softly, he said, "Rafe, that's just your wishin' side talkin'. Rance was the best of us, by God. I've seen him do stuff that no other man could do. Shoot better'n anybody, fight like nobody's business, and take six different women in a row without so much as a pause or a how-de-do."

Rafe nodded.

"But even he couldn't have lived through that," Rufus went on. "One'a them slugs went clean through his chest and out his back. As much as it kills me to think it, he's gone. Rance is dead, Rafe."

Now, Rufus had half-expected Rafe to blow up at him, to vent some of that hot, Mexican temper all over his skinny white ass, but Rafe surprised him. He started to cry.

Rufus didn't know what to do. He sat there silently for a few minutes, listening to his older brother's sobs and feeling his own throat tighten. And he wisely stayed quiet until Rafe had finished and roughly wiped his eyes on his shirtsleeve and blew his honker on his bandanna.

Then, all Rafe said to him was, "You ever tell anybody I bawled—no matter how many times I do it, you get me—I'll slit your throat, brother or not."

Although this didn't make much sense to Rufus—killing a brother because he'd seen you get all emotional over another brother's death—he nodded and said, "Sure, Rafe. I didn't see nothin'."

Silence again.

After about five minutes had passed, Rafe said, "Them gals tonight. They was fun."

"Yeah," Rufus replied. "They was, wasn't they?"

"You want some leftover beef?"

Rufus sighed. "Sure, Rafe."

"I'll bet Rance would'a liked them gals, too."

"Yeah, Rafe," Rufus replied. He could see it was going to be a long time before Rafe let go of this.

Him, too, he guessed. He wanted to see the men that had done Rance's killing dead, and in the worst way possible. He wanted them to suffer. He wanted them to scream and moan and beg for death.

But there was no sense in getting Rafe all riled up, not tonight. He'd bide his time and watch his words for now.

Once again, he said, "Yeah, I bet he would have had himself a high old time, Rafe. He sure would."

• • • •

When he'd finished his interview with Lucy, Slocum stood up from the red-cushioned chair in her red-and-pink bedroom and picked up his hat.

After talking to her, he'd decided that Lucy wasn't going to be up for any hanky panky tonight, not after what had happened to the other girls, and the men downstairs. And she was the type that would be sorely offended if he even so much as mentioned it. It was a rotten shame.

She was a real looker. Wheat-blond, fairy hair, delicate features with big brown eyes and rosebud lips, and what promised to be a voluptuous figure beneath her rather somber dress. Somber for a saloon girl, anyhow. Already he had decided that she'd look a helluva lot better out of it.

And she was damned smart. Scooting down to the cellar like that? That took quick thinking. And it had taken a lot of courage for her not to cry out when she heard those shots fired.

The rest of the fellows seemed to admire her, too.

Of course, he reminded himself that Hoopskirt was just a little three-whore town. The soiled doves probably had as high a social standing as anybody else, which, he suddenly realized, made Lucy's earlier words that much truer.

She'd said, "Just cause a girl's gotta stoop low to make a living for herself don't mean she's got no modesty or shame."

So he supposed he'd go sleep down at the livery if he had to. He didn't want to alienate Lucy, not in any way, shape or form.

She'd keep. He wanted the best possible shot at her. And oddly enough, he found himself wanting her to actually *like* him.

"Where you goin' now, Slocum?" she asked. She stood up, too. "I mean, you gonna try to get some shut-eye before you light out after those dirty skunks in the mornin'?"

He nodded. "Reckon I'll bunk down at the livery, seein' as you've got no hotel in town."

He grinned at her. "It's either that or the jail, and I ain't going back there again."

Lucy touched his arm, and he felt himself stiffen. She said, "Don't go, Slocum."

Hope bloomed eternal, he guessed. He said, "Pardon me?"

"I said, don't go. You can sleep down the hall. We've got a spare room."

Slocum sighed, and felt his britches getting loose again, damnit. He slid his hat back on his head.

Well, down the hall was better than a bed of straw, he guessed, but it was going to be awful hard to fall asleep knowing that the lovely, luscious Lucy was just a few steps up the hallway, in this very room.

In her bed, with its pink satin sheets.

Probably buck naked, too, with all that wheat-blond hair undone and fanned across the pillow and her breasts, all ripe and . . .

Shit.

"Thanks," he said, lying through his teeth. "I'd admire that."

12

Blue, who had stayed up with Frank until the wee small hours of the morning, was rudely awakened at a quarter to six the next dawn by a heavy pounding at his front door.

Wrapped in a sheet, he tripped from the bedroom, passed the parlor sofa and the grumpy but awakening Amos, and opened the door.

It was Arvil, Harry and Dutch—Tom Crisp's men. They looked like they were loaded for bear, what with the extra guns and the bandoleros slung over their shoulders, and they also looked a little perturbed to find Blue still half-asleep.

"Well, Blue?" demanded Arvil. "We goin' or not? Why ain't you ready?"

"Hold your horses, Arvil," Blue said. "Come on in while I get dressed. We had kind of a busy night around here."

"Who's he?" Arvil asked, pointing at Amos.

Before Blue had a chance to answer, Amos sat up, grimacing, and said, "A wayfaring stranger, sir." He peeked at his bandages.

"Talks funny, don't he?" Arvil said, as if Amos wasn't there at all.

"English, I reckon," ventured the hitherto silent Harry, who had walked in behind Arvil. "My pa had a feller what was English, worked for him one season. He could flop a calf offen his feet the fastest I've ever see'd."

"We British do have our talents," muttered Amos, "such as they are." And then, to Blue, he asked, "Where is Slocum?"

"Saloon," Blue replied, pulling on a fresh shirt. He only had three in total, and made certain he always had one clean one. Mrs. Ortega, who kept house for him, made sure of that.

"I imagine he had a better time of it than I did," said Amos. "In case you were wondering, your sofa is full of lumps."

Blue strapped on his gunbelt. "I wasn't, but thanks anyhow. You comin'?"

Amos, who Blue still couldn't figure out worth beans, said, "I shall meet you up at the saloon shortly, gentlemen."

Blue settled his hat on his head, then nodded to Arvil, Harry and Dutch. "Let's go, boys. I'll tell you 'bout last night on the way."

Slocum woke to the smell of fresh coffee and eggs and something sweet. Jelly?

He slitted his eyes open only to see Lucy standing over him with a tray in her hands.

"Mornin'," she said, smiling. Such a pretty smile. Such a pretty everything. "Seen the Crisp crew ridin' up toward Blue's place, and I figured I'd give you a jump on 'em."

"Thanks," said Slocum, and sat up. Lucy settled the tray across his lap. Not in time, though, to hide his morning erection.

She did look awfully fine today. And she looked awfully impressed at the big, hard lump under the sheets, too.

But neither one of them mentioned it.

As he dug into breakfast, she sat down in the chair across from him and said, "I ironed your jacket, too. It's there." She hiked a thumb toward the hook on the door. "It was awful messy."

"Thanks again," he mumbled around a mouthful of eggs. They were cooked over easy, salted and peppered just right. There was toast, too, and that sweet smell had been a pot of orange marmalade, into which he greedily stuck his knife.

"Sorry there's no bacon," she said, shrugging. "Harley won't slaughter again until next week."

Slocum smiled. "Maybe next time."

She grinned back at him. "Yeah. Next time. When you ain't in such a hurry." She looked down at her hands. "I'd . . . I'd admire to see you again, Slocum. On the house, so to speak."

She paused, and then looked up again, eyeing him humorlessly. "Don't go gettin' yourself killed out there, okay?"

As he said, "I'll try not to," she stood up and walked out the door, closing it softly behind her.

"Well, I'll be goddamned," he muttered to himself with a puzzled shake of his head. "I ought'a try not sleepin' with them the very first night more often."

Women. Who could figure them?

But she's made it clear that he was in for an extremely warm welcome if and when he got back. To say he was looking forward to it would have been an understatement. But first things first.

He gulped his coffee, finished off the toast and eggs, then dressed in a hurry, the taste of good marmalade still in his mouth. Strapping on his guns, he walked to the door and opened it just as Blue's fist, knuckles first, came toward his face.

Slocum ducked to miss it, and Blue laughed, saying, "You could give a feller a warning, you know."

Slocum stepped out into the hall. "And you could give a holler before you set into pounding on somebody's door. Jesus, Blue."

Downstairs, with the early morning sun blaring through the front windows and the bodies cleared out, Slocum was introduced to Arvil, Harry and Dutch. He also learned that Frank would recover— not that he cared much—and was at home in bed.

Slocum gauged Arvil to be a decent hand on the hunt. Harry and Dutch were likely good cowhands, he thought, but trailing human prey was likely new to them. Arvil was most likely the one they could rely on when push came to shove.

The Crisp crew seemed to have been filled in on quite a few things, from Slocum's identity to last night's activities, and Dutch even stood up when Amos walked through the doors.

"How's the side?" Slocum asked as Amos pulled up a chair.

"In the words of someone famous," Amos said dryly, "I shall live. I shall live in great pain, however." He held up a finger, and the barkeep, absent last night, rustled him up a shot of bourbon and a branch water chaser.

"You're breakin' my heart, Amos," Slocum said as Amos downed the shot.

"Good," replied Amos. "I meant to."

"Hell, I been shot worse than that six, eight times in a day," Blue said, straight-faced.

"Do tell," Amos said, his face equally expressionless.

Dutch, who hadn't said a word so far, suddenly blurted out, "Well, who the hell cares? When we gonna get after them varmints?"

Slocum stood up, throwing his long shadow across the table. "Right about now, I reckon."

•   •   •

Rufus and Rafe Carthage were already on the move, and had been since dawn. They'd spent an uncomfortable night on a bed of bare rock, and their horses, already tired and footsore, were suffering from lack of water in addition to the want of a blacksmith.

"There's a tank up ahead, if we cut north a mite," Rufus said. "I remember, from when we was through here years ago."

"You remember wrong," said Rafe.

Rafe was in an awfully bad mood this morning. Of course, he had every right to be. Just exactly what was on the top of this heap of anger was probably Rance, but Rufus wasn't about to ask. In fact, he wasn't about to even bring up their late brother's name.

"I do?" Rufus said. "Well, which way is it, then? It ought'a be good and full after last night. If it rained out here, I mean."

Rufus knew very well that in Arizona, it could thunder and pour on your right boot while your left stayed dry enough to light kindling, so he covered his bets. He was hoping that it had rained out here, though.

The horses needed a drink, and he and Rafe needed to fill their canteens. He didn't know about Rafe, but he was carrying three, and only one of them had any water in it.

Rafe simply reined his horse to the side. "South," he said. "The tank's to the south."

And that was all he said until they reached it—a large, shallow hollow in the natural bedrock—an hour later.

It was dry.

Well, dry except for a two inch-deep, squirming-with-bugs puddle about three feet across. The horses drank from it, but the Carthage boys couldn't.

"Shit," said Rufus. "Now what we gonna do?"

"I got enough water to take me to Crowfoot," Rafe announced.

Crowfoot? That was a new one on Rufus. He asked, "Where's that?"

" 'Bout twenty miles south. You comin'?"

This took Rufus by surprise. He'd never considered that they might split up. It had never so much as crossed his mind. Brothers were brothers, after all.

Carefully, he asked, "Rafe? What you mean, am I comin'?"

"Just what I said," replied Rafe, his dark eyes narrowed. "Been thinkin'. Somebody's bad luck, and I don't think it's me."

"Bad luck?" Rufus asked, his brows arched. "What?"

"Somebody got us locked up in Yuma," Rafe said. "Somebody called down those sonsabitches on us last night. Somebody lit that fire up in Payson. Somebody—"

"Rance lit that fire and you know it," Rufus broke

in. "He set that candle on the bourbon keg, not me. And I sure didn't get us caught. That was Rance, tryin' to mess with that Slocum feller. He just should'a shot him straight off, that's what, right after I killed his horse."

Amazingly, Rafe actually chuckled. "Jesus, that was funny," he said. "The damn thing just kept runnin', with its head practically hangin' off."

"Maybe it was part chicken," Rufus said, and they both got to laughing.

It lightened the mood enough that Rafe didn't again mention going on alone. In fact, he said, "Well, if you ain't got enough water, I reckon we can share. You suppose these horses have drunk enough bugs that they can go twenty miles?"

Rufus nodded. "I reckon."

Rafe mounted up, and Rufus did the same. But before they started out south, toward Crowfoot, Rufus turned in his saddle and stood in his stirrups.

"You figure they're still after us?" he asked.

Rafe shrugged. "Maybe they never were. Maybe we scared 'em off. We shot up that town pretty damn good, for what little time we had in it."

Rufus smiled. "Yeah. We did, didn't we, Rafe?"

"Just the start, little brother," Rafe said. "From now on, it's nothin' but good times and bad women and fat banks."

They rode on, Rufus bringing up the rear. As he

watched the backside of Rafe's horse moving in front of him, he hoped Rafe was right.

But still, he had one of his feelings. And it wasn't a good one.

13

About fifteen miles out of town, Blue put the brakes on.

"What now?" said Slocum.

Blue sighed. "I'm way past my authority, here, Slocum. Distance-wise. I'm a town sheriff, and my jurisdiction ended about five miles back, and that's stretchin' it. Supposed to end at the city limits."

"The hell with that, Blue!" Arvil said, and Harry and Dutch nodded in agreement. "Them bastards killed a whole batch of your citizens dead, not to mention treatin' those gals like dirt!"

"I know," said Blue. He wanted to go on, he really did, but if they caught up with those Carthage fellows, and something happened, he could be charged with murder and he knew it. "But it ain't right, me ridin' any further."

"Aw, hell, Blue," Slocum said. He looked somewhere between mad and disappointed. More mad, actually.

Amos piped up, "I do believe we should tell them, Slocum."

129

Slocum shrugged those wide shoulders of his. "Your call, Amos."

"Tell me what?" asked Blue.

Arvil and the other two echoed, "Yeah, what?"

Amos reached into his pocket and pulled out a wallet. He flipped it open, displaying a badge and an identity card. "You are all hereby authorized agents of the United States Secret Service. When we catch up with these miscreants, shoot to kill."

He snapped the wallet closed, and returned it to its hiding place.

Blue just stared at him.

Arvil said, "Slocum? He on the level?"

Slocum nodded. "He is. Don't let that Brit accent fool you. He's American through and through, and he takes his orders directly from . . . you know who. The big man in Washington."

"Holy crud," said Harry, gulping.

"The British part was just an accident of birth, I assure you," quipped Amos.

Now, this was coming just a little to fast for Blue. Not that he didn't understand the words *Secret Service* and that Amos was a part of it, but he wanted to know a little more before he went riding off into the neverlands with a bunch of men who thought they were authorized to shoot first and ask questions later.

And besides, he hadn't had too clear a look at the badge. His blue-tinted glasses messed up his near vision sometimes. No, age had messed up his near vision, he supposed, but he wasn't about to admit it.

"Now just hold on a minute," he said, raising his hand, palm out. "Lemme see that badge again." While he waited for Amos to produce it and hand it over, he asked, "Slocum, you know anything about this?"

Slocum said, "He's tellin' the truth, Blue. Wouldn't lie to you."

"I know you wouldn't," Blue said. He peered at the identification. Well, it looked real to him. Not that he was any expert. He'd never seen a Secret Service man's badge before, let alone his identification card.

He handed it back to Amos.

"So what are we, exactly?" Blue asked. "Deputies or somethin'?"

"Agents would be more proper," replied Amos.

Slocum twisted toward Amos, his saddle leather squeaking. "Yesterday, you told that Frank we were U.S. marshals."

Amos shrugged. "I thought it would be easier for the poor fellow to understand. He's not very bright, you know."

Blue's first instinct was to come to Frank's defense, except that Amos was right. Frank wasn't awfully smart. So he held his peace. He turned toward Slocum.

"I don't know Amos here for beans, but I do know you, Slocum," Blue said. "And I'd trust you with my life. Which, I reckon, is exactly what I'm doin'." He sat up a little straighter. "I'm in, until the end."

Slocum's mouth quirked up a tad. "Good man, Blue. I know you'd come. Besides," he added, reining his horse around, "I know you good enough to know that if you didn't chase these bastards down into the ground, it'd bother you up till the day you died."

"Which might be any day now," Amos cheerfully added. "For all of us, that is." He gathered his reins. "Shall we, gentlemen?"

They started out again, and from behind him, Blue heard Harry say, "Dutch, does that mean we're workin' for that crazy Englishman now?"

Arvil's voice sounded in a hiss. "No, you rock-headed idiots. It means we're workin' for the god-damn president of these United States, so you'd best do him proud!"

Blue didn't much care who he was working for. What he did care about was that now he had an excuse—a damn good one, if you asked him—for dogging those murderers to the ends of the earth.

It was enough for him.

Slocum had managed to track Rufus and Rafe Carthage over the stone because of the muddy hoof prints their horses had left behind.

They'd been clear at first, then faint, then almost nonexistent, but there were enough clues that he was able to keep going. A broken blade of grass dropped from a horse's heel here, a trail of road apples there.

He'd even discovered their "campsite" from the evening before by finding a few scraps of beef on the ground, plus their horses' waste a few yards off.

They might be keeping to the rock, but it wasn't doing them as much good as they thought it was.

He missed the place where they'd turned south, but realized his mistake in less than a quarter mile, backtracked, and found the mark of a loose horseshoe, skidding toward the south.

Good. One of them was riding a horse with a bum shoe, now. They'd be even easier to track.

He was proved right by the unmistakable, yet nearly invisible, little marks of skidding metal on stone as they followed the Carthage boys southward.

When they came to the tank, no one dismounted. It was nothing more than a buggy puddle. They simply moved on, following Rafe and Rufus farther south.

"Crowfoot," Blue said, jogging up to ride beside Slocum. "I'll bet my boots they're headed for Crowfoot."

"Ain't been there," Slocum said, as Amos rode closer, up on his other side. "What's in Crowfoot?"

"Nothin' much," Blue said, nodding at Amos to include him in the conversation. "Smaller than

Hoopskirt. Newer, too. But they got a bank that all the ranchers for miles around use."

"The cheese," said Amos.

Slocum nodded.

Blue said, "Oh, I get you. Like in a mousetrap, right?"

"Correct," Amos said. "Crowfoot it is then, gentlemen."

"I ain't so much as joggin' this horse fast until we get off this damned rock," Slocum warned. When it came down to his horse, he'd pick its welfare over just about anything.

Blue nodded. "Fair enough," and kept riding at a walk. "Wouldn't wanna throw a shoe out here."

Which was exactly what one of the Carthage boy's horses had done. A moment later, Slocum noticed it: cast to the side, a few nails still in it, and a little chunk of hoof to boot. He wondered if either one of those bastards noticed. He'd bet that the poor horse was noticing it more with every step.

"They won't be movin' too awful fast from now on," Slocum said, pointing it out to Amos and Blue.

"But we will," said Blue, and pointed ahead, toward the distance, where desert brush was growing. "We're about out of this stone."

"And glad of it," said Amos.

"Goddamn horse!" Rufus swore and lashed at his mount's neck again with the reins. He was standing in front of the animal, looking back at a hind hoof that was nearly split. "Goddamn shoe!"

"You can walk it," Rafe said.

"That's easy for you to say," Rufus snapped. He was at the end of his rope. If one more thing went wrong in his life, he swore, he'd . . . well, he didn't know. But it would be plenty mean and painful, and an awful lot of people would be sorry.

Real goddamn sorry.

"Walk it, Rufus," Rafe repeated gruffly. "It's only two more miles. You used to walk farther than that to school when you was a kid."

"When I went," Rufus said. Two miles. That was manageable. Too far to haul all his gear, though, or he would have shot the horse then and there. That foot would be ruined beyond hope by the time they walked into town.

It never occurred to him that perhaps the hoof wouldn't be so bad if he hadn't chosen to lope for miles over skittery, solid stone, or if he had thought to have his horse's feet and shoes tended to a week ago, when Rance had suggested it.

But he hadn't, and he didn't think about it. It was all the horse's fault, so far as he was concerned.

He was thirsty, for one thing. Oh, Rafe shared, but it wasn't like he offered any too often.

The first thing he wanted, when they got to Crowfoot, was a beer. Maybe two. Rafe had told him, as they rode, that Crowfoot was supposed to have a nice little bank, too, but he figured they wouldn't take that out right away.

They'd get drunk, have some women, get the town firmly under their thumbs, so to speak, and then they'd take the bank.

They'd take it easy.

And if there was a big enough take, he figured maybe they could head down to Mexico for a while.

Hoopskirt hadn't had so much as a stage stop, let alone a telegraph. It would be a spell before Slocum and his pal could get the word out to anybody. Now, Rufus figured traveling over rock for a whole day was enough to throw off anybody. There wasn't any way in the world that Slocum could be behind them.

But eventually, somebody would be.

He figured that out of the country was the safest place for him and Rafe to be. Especially if they were rich.

He hoped that bank was good and fat.

14

After Rafe put up his horse and Rufus argued with the stablehand about whether the hoof could be fixed or if he should just shoot the beast—during which the stablehand bought Rufus's horse for fifteen dollars, which sort of negated the point—they went up the street to Crowfoot's only saloon.

It wasn't as nice as the one back at Hoopskirt, having a bar which consisted of two planks tossed over the tops of a couple barrels, but it had beer, and it had girls.

Well, girl, period.

Rufus and Rafe'd had a long talk on the way into town. Well, long for them, anyway. They decided to hold themselves back as well as they could until they had time to check out the bank.

Rafe had said that you never could tell when somebody'd brought in one of these newfangled time-lock deals—one of which they had encountered several years ago up in Montana, and with which Rafe said he had no intention of dealing again.

Rufus, on the other hand, secretly figured that if

they had a choke hold on the stupid town, they could just wait out the time-lock.

But you didn't argue with Rafe, no sir, you just didn't argue with that hot Mexican temper.

So Rufus was going to try to be nice. He'd practiced on the stablehand. He hadn't killed him or anything, not even a little wound.

He thought that showed a whole lot of restraint, and he was proud of himself.

They stood at the bar, drinking their beers, while they checked the place over. Three customers besides themselves, one saloon gal with no teeth and a bad green dress, sitting by herself at a rear table, and one bored bartender, down at the far end of the splintery, six-foot "bar."

Rufus muttered, "Aw, Rafe, can't we just—"

"No," Rafe said.

"Aw, shit."

Rafe turned toward him, his dark eyes narrowed. "You mouthin' off to me, boy?"

Why had his brothers always treated him like he was their kid instead of their sibling? Why, Rafe wasn't but three years older than he was!

And Rance? Rance had been the worst. Do this, do that, go over there, come over here, lift that barge, tote that bale . . .

Rufus considered that he was getting pretty tired of this crud. He also considered that the reason he hadn't broken down and bawled when Rance got shot like Rafe had—the crybaby—was that he was actually kind of glad he wouldn't get bossed around anymore.

And now Rafe was taking over, dammit.

"Are you?" Rafe demanded. "Lippin' off?"

For just a moment, Rufus thought yeah, he was, and what was Rafe gonna do about it? But then common sense—what little he had—took hold, and he said, "Nope, Rafe. I was just commentin'."

"Well, keep your goddamn comments to yourself," Rafe growled, downed the last of his beer, then ordered a second one.

"Me, too," Rufus said. "Another beer, I mean." And he couldn't help it if his tone was a little surly.

Rafe just looked over, glaring, but didn't say anything.

Good thing, too, Rufus thought. *I'm just this close to takin' your goddamn head off.*

Meanwhile, back at Hoopskirt, which was now a town in mourning, Paul Yates, the town's combination barber/furniture maker/mortician, walked out into the shed to see about that bodies that had been brought over last night. He had a tape measure around his neck, and he wasn't in a very good mood. He'd been putting this off all day.

That Rance Carthage was sure a big sucker, mused Yates as he put his hand on the latch and brought out his key. Not tall, no sir. He reckoned

Carthage was only five-nine, five-ten, and that in his boots. But it had taken four grown men to carry him over.

Yates didn't look forward to preparing the body. He supposed he'd have to make an extra-wide casket.

And naturally, there was only the town poor fund to pay him for it. And the town poor fund was always broke, which meant, basically that he was throwing his own money down a hole after Rance Carthage.

As he turned the key in the lock, though, he smiled. He'd just remembered that Rance wasn't alone in the shed. Those other two fellers would pay for their own burials. Or at least, their families would, once Blue got back and got people notified.

That would help defray the cost somewhat.

He walked into the room, which was already smelling a little ripe, and went to the opposite window, letting up the blind and letting in the sun.

Staring out the window, his back to the three bodies lying flat on the planks that served as preparation tables, he rubbed his hands together.

"Who's to be first, gents?" Yates asked.

"Not me, you jackass," said a voice, and Yates nearly jumped out of his skin.

He whirled around to find that one of the sheeted, prone figures was prone no longer. Sitting there, big as life with a pistol pointed directly at Yates's chest, sat Rance Carthage.

"How . . . how . . . how . . . ?" Yates stuttered. "I s-saw the wounds myself! One of them went right th-through you!" He found that he was hanging onto the windowsill behind him, for the sole purpose of keeping himself upright.

"Must'a missed the important stuff," Rance barked, although a bit weakly, Yates thought with some optimism. It was a stretch to find anything at all to be optimistic about, considering the circumstances, but then, he always liked to look on the sunny side.

Part of which was that he wouldn't have to haul Rance Carthage's body around and bury it.

Maybe Rance would live just long enough to get to some other undertaker's turf.

"What happened?" Rance demanded. "Where're my brothers?" He got off the plank he was now sitting on, and ripped the sheets off the other two bodies. "You're lucky this ain't them," he said, then repeated, "Where are they?"

"T-that's sort of a long story," Yates said, tugging at his collar.

Rance leaned back, resting the bulk of his weight on the planks. He looked weak, Yates thought. Hell, he should look dead and beginning to rot, by all natural laws!

But instead, he was peeling his shirt, solid with

dried blood, away from his chest. It made a sick little ripping sound.

Rance said, "I got time." He wiggled the nose of that gun, gesturing Yates to the wooden chair in the corner.

Who the hell had brought him down here with a gun, anyway? Blue would never . . .

And then Yates remembered that Blue and those other men had lit out right away. It was Frank who had overseen the bringing down of the body.

And wasn't that just like Frank?

Yates felt his mouth tighten, just thinking about it. That Frank was too stupid to live. But then he had a happy thought. Frank might die of his wounds, yet.

Serve the sonofabitch right, if you asked him.

Rance wiggled the gun again. "Speak, gravedigger," he said.

Yates pulled a handkerchief from his pocket and mopped his brow. "Well, it's like this, Mr. Carthage. After Slocum and Sheriff Parker and Amos Marple killed you, that is to say, wounded you somewhat, they lit out after your brothers."

Rance's face wadded into a scowl. "You mean my brothers run on out me?" he nearly shouted.

Yates didn't quite know what to do, other than tell the truth. "I-I believe they both thought you had, um, expired, sir. That is, we all did. The whole town."

Rance sniffed. "Not likely." He pulled the bloody shirt away from his back, too. Again the sick, tearing sound.

Rance's chest had started to bleed again, mixing bright red and damp with the dull and rust-colored. Yates was thinking that perhaps it might be a very good idea if the fiend just bled to death right here and now.

He could manage the body by himself if need be. Certainly, he could! He could build an oversize coffin. He wouldn't even care about getting paid.

He wouldn't mind any of it, really, now that he thought about it. Because he had a feeling that unless Rance Carthage either bled to death, or at least bled enough that he passed out, Yates wasn't getting out of his own body-preparation shed alive.

"You know, you really should let me bandage those wounds for you," he said slowly, feigning concern. "Or better yet, allow me to call the doctor. I don't think you realize—"

"I realize you're stallin'," Rance said, and he looked very mean and very serious. "Get on with it, gravedigger. Tell me what the hell happened while I was out."

Swallowing hard and stuttering, Yates complied.

Rafe was upstairs with the toothless whore, and Rufus was restless. He sat at a corner table, all alone, sipping his fourth beer and grinding his teeth.

He'd taken about all of this he was going to take. First, a lifetime of crud from Rance, and now what promised to be the same thing from Rafe. Hell, when he was fifty Rafe would still be bossing him around and telling him what to do.

When Rafe had first go at the only whore in town, that was just about the last straw. Rafe was goddamn lucky that Rufus hadn't shot him on the spot, that's all he had to say.

He felt like going down to the livery and shooting his goddamn horse, just because. And then maybe he'd shoot that stableman that bought the gelding, too. Folks needed to learn that Rufus Carthage wasn't a man to be trifled with!

No, Rafe was the one who needed that lesson.

He stared out the front windows, a nasty expression on his face and even nastier thoughts running through his head, when he saw a pretty girl standing right across the street.

She was alone. That was good. And of course, she was pretty, at least from this distance. That was better. Better than that toothless whore any day.

Without a further thought of Rafe or anything he'd said about laying low or casing the bank or waiting his turn for the whore, Rufus stood up, stretched his arms nonchalantly and walked outside.

Quickly, he checked both ways. The street was close to deserted, and the sidewalks as well. The girl was still across the way, looking into the display window of a dressmaker's shop.

He crossed the street.

Slowly, he walked up to her.

She didn't look at him. She didn't seem to know he was there.

You will in a minute, honey, he thought.

He came up and stopped right next to her. She was blond, and she was wearing some kind of pretty scent, like lemons.

He took off his hat and said, "Howdy, ma'am. How you doin' today?"

She turned toward him, annoyed, he supposed, that a strange man would speak to her on the street. Women sure had some funny ideas. Even girls. He figured her for about seventeen.

Without a word, she turned on her heel and walked away.

He followed.

And when she came to the first alley, he quickly checked the streets again, then took three long, fast steps to catch her.

In an instant, her mouth was covered by his dirty hand. He lifted her by the waist, and pulled her, struggling wildly, into the mouth of the alley.

"That's right," he whispered. "That's right, missy. I like it when gals fight me."

He pinned the terrified girl to the wall with one arm, and still managing to cover her mouth, he yanked and ripped at her dress, tearing it half away.

He smiled. She had real nice tits.

"Yeah, honey," he muttered to the struggling girl as he quickly unbuttoned his trousers. "Keep it up. I like it fine."

He took her against the wall, all the time covering her hysterical screams and cries with his hand. It didn't take long. He was that randy.

And when he was finished, he simply snapped her neck to shut her up.

He buttoned himself up. Then, keeping an eye to the street, he stuffed the body, half-naked, bruised and bleeding, back behind some barrels and packing crates and threw a little excess excelsior over it.

Straightening his hat, he walked back across the street to the saloon and sat back down at his table. He picked up his beer again.

Nothing had changed, except for that little girl out there, hidden behind some barrels. Nobody had moved, nobody was the wiser.

And, he thought with a smile, she'd been pretty, even up close. Cute little spray of freckles right across her nose. Blue eyes, too. At least, he thought they'd been blue. Might have been blue-gray.

Anyhow, she'd been a whole lot better-looking than that whore Rafe had, and he'd popped her, too, broke her in. He could tell by the thin skin of blood on his cock when he was finished.

Ha! Let Rafe chew on that for a while!

15

Slocum, being in the lead, found it first. He reined Sonny, his oddly colored Appy, to a sliding stop and stared down at the ground.

"We've got 'em, boys," he said. Rather like the cat who'd caught the canary, Amos thought. There were practically feathers sticking out the sides of Slocum's mouth.

Amos and Blue looked down, too. It was clear to Amos as well. Here, the horse that had limped for miles, the horse that had lost a shoe, had finally given out. The print from the near right hoof was misshapen, for it had most likely split partially, and now the rider was set afoot.

When Amos looked up, Blue was smiling, an expression shared by Arvil, Harry and Dutch. They all knew they weren't too very far from their quarry now. They all knew it was just a matter of time, perhaps minutes.

However, Amos was a tad concerned, and it looked as if his old friend Slocum was, too. Slocum stared off into the distance, then pulled out his spyglass and looked through it for a long time.

At last, he folded it up and put it away. "It's clear," he said. "For a good distance, anyhow. Blue, how far are we from Crowfoot?"

Blue shrugged. "Mile or two. Two and a half at the outside. It's just below that hill on the horizon, as I recall" he said, pointing. "I ain't been down this way for a spell."

They took off again at a jog, then slowly moved up into a lope, each man keeping an eye on the distant hills and the horizon, over which they hoped to find the Carthage brothers.

When Rance Carthage left the body-preparation shed, he left Yates behind, dead and covered with a sheet on the planks that Rance had formally occupied.

He knew what had happened now, he thought as he saddled Yates's horse. He knew what those fools, Rafe and Rufus, had done, and in which direction the posse had taken out after them.

Chances were, Rufus and Rafe were dumb enough to figure they'd lost that posse. But Rance knew that sonofabitch Slocum and his bastard buddy, Amos Marple, didn't give up that easy. When the Carthages were in Yuma Prison, more than one inmate had confided in him that Slocum was the best "bumblebee through a blizzard" tracker than ever was.

Rance didn't care how much bedrock rose up to

the surface to ring Hoopskirt, or how much it rained or didn't rain. That bastard, Slocum, would track those idiots down, or die trying.

Rance hoped it was the latter. But he had no time to waste on those pleasant thoughts.

He led out another of Yates's horses, one of a matched pair of blacks—this one probably a coach horse for pulling the ebony and gilt, glass-sided, fancy-plumed hearse parked out back—and clipped a lead rope to its halter.

"You'd best be saddle-broke," he grumbled to it as he mounted the other, a dun. "If'n you ain't, you're sure gonna be by the time I get done with your lazy, goddamn ass."

The Yates Furniture, Barber Shop, and Undertaking Establishment was on the edge of town, surrounded by a grove of palo verde. Rance was confident that no one saw him as he quietly left town, riding the dun and leading the black.

He was also confident that no one saw him break into a canter once he got clear of town and picked up the posse's trail.

His shoulder pained him something fierce, his side throbbed, and his chest hurt like a bastard. He hadn't sought out the doc, though. He'd simply bandaged himself up the best he could, after downing a couple shots of whiskey and digging out the slug still caught in his shoulder and the other in his side.

Those last two stung like angry beestings, partly because of the extra whiskey he'd poured into the newly raw flesh, but the worst was his chest.

He was pretty sure that particular slug hadn't hit anything vital. Like he'd told the undertaker, he was breathing, wasn't he? Still, he could feel that it had sure done some kind of damage on its way through.

But he didn't have time for rest or fussing, or even thinking about it. He had to find those peckerwood brothers of his before they stirred up a hornet's nest they couldn't swat and shoot their way out of.

Either that, or he'd have to ferret out that goddamn posse and take care of them before they had a chance to get at his brothers.

One way or the other, he was going to beat Rafe senseless when he found him.

Rafe should have taken charge, and he should've known better. The sonofabitch should've known that a little thing like three slugs wasn't enough to kill Rance Carthage.

And even if Rafe—or Rufus—was dumb enough to buy into that—and it appeared that they had been exactly that stupid—they should have known better than to ride right back into the same town.

Idiots. Fools!

He had a couple of certified knuckleheads for brothers.

He lashed at the buckskin, then yelled at the black

to move its sorry ass, and galloped off in a generally southward direction, the black trailing behind.

Rufus, fairly drunk by this time, was down in the bar, nursing his sixth beer, when he saw his brother starting down the steps from his rendezvous with the toothless whore.

He stared stupidly as Rafe, with a satisfied look plastered all over his Mexican face, crossed the room and pulled out a chair.

"Told her you'd be up directly," Rafe said, and signaled to the barkeep, indicating a beer, and to hurry up about it.

"She's pretty good," he continued. "I like them ones with no teeth, if you know what I mean." His elbow jabbed Rufus's side.

Rufus shrugged away, spilling his beer in the process. "Don't want your sloppy seconds," he grumbled. And then, for God only knows what reason, he smugly added, "Already had some'a my own."

Rafe's eyes narrowed. "You what?"

"Told you."

Rafe's face darkened. "Listen, you drunken fool," he began in a low but very serious voice, "if you done anything to louse this—"

"Penny?" called a voice from the street, and they both looked out the window. "Penny! Coltrane, I've lost her!"

The speaker was a middle-aged man, a farmer or

a rancher come to town for supplies, and he was gesturing to a man who could only be the town sheriff. Metal glinted on his chest.

Clear across the street, they heard the rancher shout, "Don't tell me not to worry! I been everywhere lookin'. I tell you, she's disappeared!"

Rufus began to get kind of a queasy feeling in the pit of his stomach.

Rafe glared at him. "Don't suppose you know anythin' about that, out there?" he said softly.

Rufus leaned back in his chair, trying to bluff it out. "Mayhap I do, mayhap I don't."

"You shit-for-brains cob-head!" Rafe muttered, and grabbed Rufus's arm, jerking him forward, then to his feet.

The sudden gain in altitude kind of threw the half-drunken Rufus, and it took him a half-second to get his bearings again. When he did, he shouted, "What the hell do you think you're doin'?"

It was the wrong thing to say and the wrong time—and the wrong man—to say it to.

Waving off the bartender bringing his beer, Rafe steered Rufus outside, then down the walk.

"Where the Sam Hill we goin'?" Rufus demanded, although he was sozzled enough that it came out all slurry and didn't have nearly the sarcastic punch he intended it to.

"The livery," Rafe said tersely.

"But we just come from there!" Rufus argued.

He wanted to go and see whether that bank had a time-lock or not. He hoped it didn't. He was in the mood to stick it up right now, and they could start off by shooting that sheriff, Coltrane.

He was sure handy enough. Hell, he was just back there a half a block!

But Rafe kept on tugging at him, yanking him like a little kid who's gonna get a whipping when he gets home, and it suddenly occurred to him that he didn't have to take this.

He could get mad, by God! He could just plain refuse.

He put on the brakes, the dust skidding up in little clouds behind his heels, and defiantly said, "Ain't goin'."

"Yeah, you are," Rafe insisted, and damned if he didn't have that woodshed look on his face, just like their pa used to get.

"No," insisted Rufus. "I wanna go rob the damn bank now!"

"Shut yourself up or I'll do it for you," Rafe hissed. "Jesus Christ! Just when I think you're half-way growed up, you go actin' like a stupid kid again!"

"I ain't no kid!"

"Then stop actin' like it!"

It occurred to Rufus that this conversation could go on until sometime after dark, and probably would—neither brother willing to give an inch—

when someone cried out, back up the street.

It was a man's cry of shock and horror, and Rufus knew exactly what had caused it.

Suddenly he said, "Y'know, you're right, Rafe. Let's get ourselves down to the—"

"Oh, God!" came the cry again. "Penny, my Penny! What have they done to you?"

"Aw, shit," Rafe mumbled as they hurried down the street.

Rufus glanced behind him just long enough to see a smallish crowd gathering at the mouth of the alley where he'd hidden the girl's body.

"A blanket, somebody get a blanket to cover my poor dead girl," he heard the man cry out, and there were literally tears in his voice.

Some fellows were such babies about stuff, Rufus though scornfully. She was only a girl, after all. Dime a dozen.

"Hurry up!" Rafe hissed, and yanked him through the livery door.

They cut out of town at a fast gallop, leaving behind their original horses and a stableman with a pitch-fork through his heart. All because he'd objected when they started to saddle up a couple of fresh mounts that didn't exactly belong to them.

It was all the stableman's fault, really, Rufus thought as he struggled to keep his balance on the galloping horse. It was his own fault he'd ended up skewered on his own pitchfork.

If the man had kept a knife around the stable, Rufus wouldn't have had to use the pitchfork.

And naturally, Rafe wouldn't let him fire his gun. Too much noise, he'd said.

There Rafe went again, giving him those god-damn orders, Rufus had thought after they led the horses outside. If it hadn't been for the angry mob coming down the street right straight for them, Rufus would have given Rafe what for, that's what.

They were a couple miles out of town, now, and Rafe slowed up a little. Rufus followed his lead gratefully. It had been all he could do to hang on.

He chanced a glance behind them.

Nobody was there. Not even a distant cloud of hoof-raised dust.

Rufus took it upon himself to rein his mount down to a walk. The horse was grateful, but Rafe wasn't.

"What the hell you doin'?" he shouted angrily. "Come on!"

"No earthly sense in runnin' when there ain't no-body chasin' us," Rufus said, in what he hoped was his most sagely voice.

Rafe took off his hat and smacked him across the face with it.

"Hey!" sputtered Rufus. His eyes stung now, and he thought he was bleeding where one of the conchos on Rafe's hat band had caught him.

Roughly, Rafe tugged his hat back on. "You beat everything, you know that? I swear, I don't know how the hell Rance kept you from takin' the bit in your teeth half the time. If you wasn't my brother—my onlyest brother, now—I swear, I'd kill you myself!"

Rufus sat up straight in the saddle, although he weaved a tad. "Go on, you half-beaner sombitch. Try. I dare you."

"Jesus," muttered Rafe, and snatched off his hat again.

Rufus ducked unconsciously, but this time, the hat wasn't aimed at him. Rafe smacked Rufus's horse on the butt, and it sprang into a lope.

Rufus nearly went off, but he managed, however clumsily, to stick to the saddle.

And then Rafe rode up next to him and smacked his horse again!

There was going to be some kind of showdown when they finally stopped to camp, Rufus thought, vomiting stale beer all down his chest and side. Yes, sir, some kind of showdown.

As soon as he stopped puking.

16

Slocum and company rode into Crowfoot to find a town in mourning.

While Blue went off to talk to the sheriff, and Arvil huddled with Harry and Dutch, softly arguing back and forth, Slocum said to Amos, "We missed 'em. Again, goddammit."

"Not by too long, I don't believe," Amos said as they walked into the saloon. "A couple of beers, if you don't mind, sir," he said to the bartender, then added, "When did those miscreants ride out of town?"

The barkeep slid two beers to them, and asked angrily, "Them assholes what killed poor Penny Springer? Who wants to know?"

"Posse, out of Hoopskirt," Amos said smoothly. "Our sheriff's talking to yours as we speak."

"What'd they do in Hoopskirt?"

"Killed and raped and made a general nuisance of themselves," Amos said with a shrug.

"Well, they did the same here," the bartender said with a scowl. "Did poor little Penny awful bad. Just standin' on the street, she was! And then they stabbed Orv Kenrick, down at Kendrick's Livery, with his own damn pitchfork. Stole two horses, too!" The man turned his head and spat on the floor. "I hope you hang 'em, and that they die real slow."

"You didn't send out a posse of your own?" Slocum asked.

"Ain't been time yet!" the bartender said. "Only been a half hour since they went gallopin' south, out of town, like the cowards they was."

"A half hour?" Slocum asked, his eyebrows shooting up.

Amos took a quick gulp of his beer, then tossed a few coins on the bar. While they still spun, he nodded to Slocum. "Shall we?"

Slocum simply nodded and started toward the doors. They were close, very close. Their horses were tired and the Carthage boys had fresh mounts, but they could catch them, Lord willing.

Except that when he and Amos walked outside, they ran right into Arvil and the other two. Arvil had his hat off, which didn't bode well as far as Slocum was concerned.

"What?" he said.

"We been talkin'," Arvil began. "About these fellers we're chasin'. And about other stuff, too. See, we don't figure that old Tom, God rest him, would want us to go clear to Mexico to run down his killers. We figure he'd probably say to come on back and get busy tendin' to his ranch."

"We got cows to round up," said Harry.

"And horses to break," added Dutch.

"And those last two Carthage boys are only a half hour ahead of us," Slocum said, gruffly. "You gonna quit on us now?"

Arvil looked at his boots. Harry and Dutch simply looked away.

"All three of you?" Slocum demanded.

"I'm goin' home," said Harry.

"Me, too," echoed Dutch.

But Arvil looked up again. "Only a half hour, you say?"

Amos nodded in the affirmative.

"Well, I reckon I'm still in, then," Arvil said. "I was Tom's foreman, and I reckon it's sort of my place to see his killers put down." He turned toward his men. "You fella's, go on back and see to young Trey. Ain't no shame in it."

"You swear, Arvil?" asked Dutch.

"Swear to God," Arvil replied, crossing his chest with a finger. Slocum had to grudgingly admire the way he was handling this. Arvil continued, "Go on, now, fellers. Those critters need tendin', and young Trey can't do it all by hisself."

"Who's Trey?" Amos asked.

Arvil said, "Old Tom's grandson. Reckon he's the boss now. He wanted to come along, but we wouldn't let him. He's only sixteen, you know?"

Slocum said, "We're wastin' daylight, fellers. Do

what you're gonna do, but do it quick. We'll probably pick up some locals." He started toward the sheriff's office.

Amos kept step with him. "Do you honestly think, my dear Slocum, that we're going to find any volunteers for the posse in this little hamlet?"

"Course not," Slocum replied stoically. "But Harry and Dutch had their minds set on goin' back. I don't want a man along who ain't keen on the idea of blowin' Rafe and Rufus Carthage directly to Hell. Don't need a couple of ranch hands who're worried about their stock more than savin' their skins."

"Or ours," Amos added.

"Right."

Rance Carthage had discarded the dun, and was now riding the black. He'd made excellent time so far, and he figured to be about ten miles out of Crowfoot. That was the only town they could be headed for.

The tracks of a whole posse were a lot easier to follow than the tracks of two riders, even over stone, and he had a fairly easy time of it.

The going wasn't so easy with his wounds, though. The shoulder and the side, they'd stopped paining him so much, but his chest? That was a different matter.

It was hurting more, a real deep hurt, all the time, and it was beginning to really worry him.

Not that he'd admit it to himself. So far as he was concerned, he was invincible, unkillable, totally unstoppable, and he'd live to be a hundred and ten. He was the strongest man he'd ever had the pleasure to know, both physically and mentally, and he figured that would always stand him in good stead.

He was certainly luckier in those respects—head and body—than his brothers. The fools.

He found himself pushing his pain aside by picturing what Rafe was going to look like, once he caught him up and beat the tar out of him.

He might just pummel Rufus, too, just to teach him a lesson that he wouldn't forget. Like, for instance, never count your brother out until you see him buried.

Maybe not even then.

He gave the black another lash with the ends of his reins, and hunkered low in the saddle.

He meant to catch up to that posse first and take them out for good and all, especially Slocum and that sonofabitch limey, Amos Marple.

And then he'd see to his brothers.

Blue shrugged again, and with disgust filling his voice, said, "They're not comin', Slocum. Not even the sheriff. I tried to talk him into it, but no go. Hell, even the girl's daddy—the little gal what got raped and killed—won't come. The doc's got him sedated over at the boarding house, anyhow." He spat to one side. "Goddamn sheriff. Pisses me off."

Slocum said, "We lost Harry and Dutch, too. It's gettin' down to it, I guess." He didn't look upset, only a little annoyed.

Blue, who had taken off his tinted glasses while he was inside, talking with Crowfoot's Sheriff—so-called sheriff, anyhow—Coltrane, gave them a rub on his sleeve, then settled them back on his nose.

The sun was awful bright today, but that wouldn't be a problem in a couple of hours. The sun was headed toward the horizon.

He said, "Where'd Amos get to?"

Slocum said, "He's pickin' up a few extra supplies. Just in case. I don't want to give those boys another chance to get away again. They've slipped through my fingers two times. Once in Hoopskirt and now again in Crowfoot. No way that I'm lettin' that happen again, Blue."

Blue nodded and they began walking back down the street toward Arvil, and their tethered horses, minus Harry's sorrel and Dutch's bay. They were long gone. Blue watched as Amos came up the street, slipped a slim parcel into his saddlebags, and struck up a conversation with Arvil.

"Where you know him from, Slocum?" Blue asked. "Amos, I mean."

"A long time back," Slocum replied. "Actually, since just after the War. We sort of worked together for a while. Lost track of him until a few years back.

That was when we rounded up these peckerwoods the first time. Jury should'a hung 'em, but they didn't." He stopped and shook his head. "Guess God wasn't watchin' that day. So, here we are again."

That answered some of Blue's questions, but not all of them, not by a long shot. But just then they joined the others. Someone—most likely Arvil— had refilled their water bags and canteens, he noticed, and Amos was just tightening his horse's cinch.

"Ready, gentlemen?" Amos asked.

"Yup," replied Slocum as he saw to his horse, then swung up. "You get what you wanted?"

"Indeed," Amos said.

Blue was busy checking over his roan. Crackerjack looked rested enough, considering all the miles he'd covered today. He figured the horses had been standing for a good half hour. It wasn't ideal, but it was enough.

He was the last to mount up.

Slocum gathered his reins. "All right, boys. It's just us, now. We're gonna pace these horses to get the most out of 'em. Much as I want to see those Carthages dead in a ditch, I sure don't want to lame my horse. They ain't that far ahead, and they're gonna have to stop eventually. When they do, we'll have 'em."

"Precisely my thoughts, old chap," Amos piped up cheerily.

Arvil didn't say anything. He was likely wondering what it felt like for Harry and Dutch, to be going home. But Blue said, "Let's do it."

At a jog, they rode out of town.

The black had about given out, and Rance was wishing he'd hung onto the dun instead of turning it loose. But he was only about three miles from Crowfoot now. Only about three miles from hopefully catching up with either the posse or his brothers, or both.

He hadn't caught sight of either group so far, even at the quick pace he was traveling. But he was confident, by God. Confident that he'd catch them, and confident that he'd kill his brothers' pursuers, and confident that he'd teach his goddamned, peckerwood brothers a lesson they'd never forget.

The black was showing marked signs of distress by the time he had ridden another mile closer to Crowfoot, and so he was encouraged to see a couple of riders, proceeding at a slow jog, coming toward him.

He slowed down before they had a chance to glimpse him, and reined his horse behind the cover of a few scrubby bushes.

They were turning now, coming straight toward him, and he quickly dismounted, gripping unconsciously at his chest as he did.

He slid his rifle from its boot, then knelt down in his horse's shade. And waited.

It didn't take long. They rode into range, and he let them come even farther before he raised the rifle to his shoulder. The horses might run too far to catch, otherwise.

He set his sights on the man riding the bay.

And then, when the time was right, he squeezed the trigger. Before there was time to see whether his slug had hit home, he changed his target to the man on the sorrel, and squeezed again, just as the fellow on the bay slid off his horse.

The second man appeared to hear the first shot after his friend fell, and suddenly turned his head. In shock and surprise, Rance supposed.

But it was too late. Rance's bullet took him square through the heart, and he, too, slithered and slid to the ground.

Only then did he look toward the first man. He frowned. Too high. The shot hadn't hit him smack in the chest, but it had gone right through the neck.

Well, whatever worked, worked.

Their horses just stopped. Didn't wander off or anything. Rance smiled despite the pain in his chest. He liked a well-trained animal.

He sat there a moment longer, watching for any signs of movement. When he had watched for about five minutes and the men still lay still, he stood up and mounted the sweating black again.

Gripping his chest, he slowly rode down to pick up his new horses.

17

"Cain't we hurry up just a little bit?" Arvil complained. "They're gonna get away from us, I'm tellin' you!"

"No," said Slocum, Blue and Amos, all at once, and a surprised Arvil gave a little jump back in his saddle.

Amos said, "Now, see here. There's no need to run these horses into the ground just to catch up with them sooner than later. We'll corner them tonight, either way. You'll have plenty of chances to take your revenge, old chap, never fear."

"I'm just afraid it's gonna get too dark for us to spy out their trail," Arvil still protested. "What if we lose 'em entire?"

"Arvil?" said Slocum, who had gone through this with him before, as had they all.

"What?" Arvil replied.

"Shut up."

Arvil grumbled for a moment, then said, "I might as well have rode back home with Dutch and Harry. I sure ain't gonna see no justice done with you boys tonight. Maybe not never."

"Yes, Arvil," said Amos airily. "That's right. Look on the bright side."

"Aw, you shut up, too," Blue suddenly broke in. "I'm gettin' real tired of all'a Arvil's bitchin' and Amos's snide remarks. None'a which Arvil gets. So as far as I can tell, Amos is makin' 'em for his own damned amusement."

"What don't I get?" Arvil demanded.

Slocum stopped grinding his teeth long enough to shout, "Enough! Y'know, once upon a time—like about an hour ago—I would'a said we'd be better off without Arvil, but now I'm beginnin' to think I'd be better off without the lot of you. Now, stop your bitchin'! These are the goddamned Carthages we're out after, not some bunch of kids who ran off with the church poor box. These are cold-blooded killers with no compunctions at all. You three forgettin' that little fact?"

"Compunctions," repeated Amos softly. "Excellent word choice, Slocum."

Blue didn't hear and Slocum pretended not to, lest it get Blue started again.

Arvil, at least, had the sense to stare at his hands, but Blue said, "And you'll pardon me all to hell, but how come you're in charge, there, Slocum? I thought this was Mr. Fancy Britches's party." Curtly, he nodded toward Amos.

"Ah, my friends," Amos said wearily, with a shake of his head. "We're all tired, gentlemen. Our horses are tired, our backsides are tired, and most of all, I'm tired of arguing and wresting about over nothing. I suggest we save our copious latent belligerence for Rufus and Rafe Carthage, who are undoubtedly not far from here."

Then Amos turned in his saddle and continued, "Blue, if my tone has offended you, I am heartily sorry. I'm afraid it's my way, and I can't change it. Arvil, believe me, I understand your frustration, and I sympathize with it. And while our friend Slocum may not be officially in charge, I would personally follow him through the gates of hell, if need be."

"Thanks, Amos," Slocum said with a curt nod.

"Not a problem," replied Amos.

"Jesus Christ on a crutch," muttered Blue.

Slocum ignored him, and added, "And now we can pick up a little speed, Arvil. The horses have had a break. But keep it to a slow lope, and stay behind me."

Arvil said, "Thank God," but the sound was somewhat muffled by the noise of hoofbeats kicking up, kicking into the rhythm of a slow canter.

Rufus and Rafe had left behind a clean trail, and an easy one to follow, Slocum thought as he loped along. They hadn't taken the time to try to hide it or do anything cagey. They'd just taken off, and taken off fast.

Of course, Slocum wasn't sure if they were capable of anything cagey, what with Rance dead, now. All in all, he had a pretty good feeling that they would catch and corner Rafe and Rufus tonight, and kill them, one way or the other. Case closed, as Amos would say.

But still, something was gnawing at the back of his brain, something indefinable, something cryptic, and he couldn't get rid of the feeling.

But he was so close, so goddamn close! So he just decided, for now, to ignore that feeling. He'd deal with it later.

When Rance Carthage rode down into Crowfoot, he didn't quite get the welcome he was expecting, and he'd been expecting just about anything: a shootout with the Hoopskirt posse, a rampage with his brothers, the bank in the process of being held up, the whole place in an uproar, you name it.

He didn't expect, however, to be backed out of the bar at the point of two rifles and a Greener shotgun, just because he was a stranger and he had red hair.

He didn't expect the populace at large to pelt him with wizened apples and eggs and tomatoes and cabbages and road apples.

He didn't expect that he'd have to get back on his stolen bay, cowering and ducking vegetables and fruit and horse shit, and ride out of town at a lope, leading the sorrel.

And he also didn't expect, once he got far enough

out of throwing range, that he'd turn around, pull his rifle from the boot, and shoot down three citizens in cold blood before making his getaway.

Although out of everything that happened, that was probably the most like Rance.

Those numbskull brothers of his must have made some kind of impression on Crowfoot, all right!

It had never crossed Rance's mind that there was anything odd about his own appearance, that he might make a frightening first appearance. He'd forgotten about the dried and fresh blood soaked through and nearly covering his shirt, and the burnt and frayed gunshot holes through it.

Of course, he'd almost forgotten about the pain, too, in his sure and certain nearness to finding his brothers once more. He had to find that damned posse first, though, that was the thing. He had to put those bums in hell once and for all.

And he would, he thought as he followed their trail. He would.

Anytime now.

And once he'd taken care of that business—along with a visit to the proverbial woodshed for his pea-brained brothers—well, the highfalutin town of Crowfoot need to be taught a little lesson, too.

Yes, indeed, they did.

He smiled at that, and hurried on.

* * *

"Get down," Slocum hissed, and motioned the others off their mounts before they caught up with him.

He was already on the ground.

He waited for them on the top of a shallow rise, after shooing his Appy away. It wandered back down the slope and started to graze along with the others.

He was kneeling when they caught up to him.

"There," he said to no one in particular, and pointed.

There, in the little basin of land, sheltered from the wind by nothing but living rock and sand dunes and what brush was able to cling to life there, sat a little cabin. It was built out of smooth stone and raw rock. There was a light in the window, and a fire in the chimney.

There were also two bodies lying out in the yard. Two men, middle-aged, it looked like.

Hard to tell in the dark, especially when they were in the shadows of the rock cabin and the big stone stock tank.

Blue, who was glass-less by this time, thumbed back his hat and breathed, "Shit."

Amos said nothing, but Slocum knew his feelings on the subject were just about the same as Blue's.

Arvil swallowed hard, then whispered, "Holy God. We gotta stop this before it goes any further."

"As we've been saying all afternoon," Amos muttered as he checked his guns. He'd come up the hill loaded for bear, looked like.

"So what do we do now?" Arvil asked. "Just start in to blastin' 'em?"

"Gotta make sure it's them, first," Blue said. He, too, was making a last check of his weapons. "After all, somebody might have come along after 'em."

"And might have been too distraught to at least cover those bodies?" Amos asked.

Blue gave him a dirty look. "Maybe," he snapped. "I don't know about the United States Secret Service, but us fellers out here in the front lines got to be careful about folks."

"Knock it off," Slocum grumbled. "Arvil, take the left flank. Blue, the right. Me and Amos'll stay put and try to coax 'em out."

Blue skittered off one way and Arvil went in the opposite direction.

Slocum muttered, "Amos, I'm gonna have to kill you one'a these days."

"Not just yet, if you don't mind, old chap," Amos said. "Let's get this little thing out of the way first. Now, may I ask how you propose to coax them to the forefront?"

Slocum didn't answer. Instead, he turned his head toward the little rock cabin and hollered, "Rufus! Rufus and Rafe Carthage! You in there?"

A flurry of shots exploded from the cabin, and Amos and Slocum both ducked back behind the crest of the hill just in time to avoid the sand and gravel kicked up by their impact.

"Golly," said Amos dryly. "I wish I'd thought of that. So very subtle."

Arvil and Blue were firing by this time, laying down slugs all over the cabin, but mostly in the general direction of the windows. The bullets coming from Blue's direction were having better luck finding their target, but nobody had yelped from inside, yet.

Stone shattered and chipped from the little building as Slocum and Amos popped up over the rim again and began to fire.

"Somethin' tells me we ain't gonna shoot through that rock any time soon," Slocum said over the exploding gunfire.

"Just what I was thinking," Amos replied. He reached down the hill a few feet, to his saddlebags, which he'd brought along. "The roof, you think?"

"Be my best guess," Slocum answered. "Looks to be thatched straw."

Amos nodded, reached inside the saddlebag's pocket, and pulled out a stick of dynamite.

He smiled a little. "Just like that first little job we did together, back outside Omaha."

"Worked then, as I recall," Slocum replied. "Course, you can never tell with Carthages."

Amos struck a lucifer while Slocum shouted, "Hold your fire! Hold your fire, men!"

From the side, he heard Arvil shout, "Who you talkin' to?"

Slocum rolled his eyes, and called back, "You, you idiot. Everybody. The cabin, too."

Eventually, the men in the cabin stopped shooting at them, although it took long enough that Amos had to shake out his first match and blow on his singed fingers. "Can we just get on with it, please?" he hissed as he pulled a fresh lucifer from his tin.

"Gotta make Blue happy," Slocum whispered back. And then he shouted, "Hello the cabin!"

There was a pause, and then somebody—probably Rufus, Slocum thought—shouted back, "What you want, you shit-ass law dogs?"

Beside Slocum, it was Amos's turn to roll his eyes.

Slocum ignored it. He called, "Come out now, with your hands empty and over your heads."

In reply came another volley of shots from the cabin. Blue and Arvil started returning it as fast as they could.

"Well," said Amos, striking the match on his gun belt, "Lord knows you tried. Magnificent effort, old friend."

"Thanks," Slocum said dryly. "Just light and throw, will you?"

"My pleasure."

With a fiery blue pop and hiss, Amos touched the match to the fuse. He waited a moment, watching it burn down a tad. Then he got to his feet and drew his pitching arm back. Slocum covered his ears.

But before there was time for the dynamite to explode, Amos fell. Fell right down in a heap next to him, and Slocum had to scramble fast to get the explosives out of his hand and tossed aside.

As it was, the dynamite only rolled down into the yard, blowing up the stock tank and sending bits of stone and metal and a great deal of water up in the air.

Slocum was too busy to notice, though. He moved to Amos, cursing the Carthage brothers the whole time, and turned him over. Amos was alive, but there was no slug hole he could see.

And then he had an awful bad thought. He rolled his unconscious friend to the side, and there it was: a hole in his back, just down a tad from the top of his left shoulder.

He stared out into the darkness behind him. *Who in the hell was out there?*

18

Amos halfway regained consciousness almost immediately, and Slocum heard him exclaim, "Bloody Hell! Have I been shot?"

Only Amos could say those words with such umbrage and outrage, and Slocum couldn't help but let a hint of a smile cross his face. But that was all he had time for. The gun battle was still raging, in fits and spurts after a small pause for everybody to be taken aback by the explosion.

He said, "Yeah, Amos. In your back. We've got an uninvited guest out there, somewhere."

Slocum scanned the surrounding territory the best he could. It was mostly moon-silvered brush, no trees, and very gently rolling.

"He could be anywhere," Amos said, echoing Slocum's thoughts.

"Shut up," Slocum growled. "You're losin' blood."

"Well, most people do, after they've been shot," Amos replied through gritted teeth. "I don't see why I should be any—"

Another shot sounded from behind them, just as

the grit, inches from Slocum's side, popped up with the impact.

Amos began, "I suggest we—"

"Move!" Slocum shouted, and dragged Amos to one side over into the cover of bushes. It wasn't a very good place to shoot from, but it was a fair to middlin' hiding place.

Blue and Amos were still firing sporadically, and Slocum heard a familiar bird call. It was Blue, signaling a question, if he remembered right. He wanted to know what the hell was going on.

Slocum whistled back after a second. He hoped he'd just signaled that there was trouble. Either that, or he'd sent the message that the U.S. Cavalry was on its way.

It had been a long time.

Inside the stone cabin, Rafe's face was full of rock chips, which he sat on the floor, picking out, while Rufus kept up firing from a window.

"Slow the hell down!" Rafe growled as he plucked out another shard. "You're gonna run us out of ammo."

Rufus, who was bleeding, too, just kept firing. He'd had about enough of being ordered around. After all, he'd wanted to keep on going, not stop here for the night. He would have been just as happy to ride around both those old coots instead of kill them and take their cabin.

But no, Rafe had to have his way, and they'd wasted a couple-three slugs on them, then got themselves trapped in here. Just like a couple of goddamn rats.

He couldn't figure out why the fellows in the center had stopped firing. Maybe they'd got them. Now, there was a happy thought! But the boys on either side were keeping him busy enough.

He was glad the cabin had been built of stone. No slug could make its way through to get at him, that was for sure! But these bullets singing off the window's edge, that was another matter. He had to keep wiping his face to keep the blood out of his eyes. And it hurt, goddamm it, when he accidentally rubbed one of those stone fragments the wrong way.

"Will you get back to your post, dammit?" he yelled at Rafe. That was another thing about stone cabins. Sound echoed through them like nobody's business. When that blast had gone off it had almost deafened both of them!

At least they'd only thrown the one, so Rufus figured that meant it was the only one they had. He felt better about that, but oddly disappointed that he hadn't thought of it first, hadn't thought to bring along a little dynamite of his own. That would have been some sight, all right, seeing those men and their mounts blown straight to hell!

Rafe was getting up off the floor and crawling to the other window at long last. Rufus watched as

Rafe crouched under the opening, checked his rifle and handgun again, then brought up the rifle and began firing.

Finally. For a change, somebody was taking *his* orders!

In the distance, Rance had just finished a long string of rather inventive swear words.

He squatted back down in the brush, seething, but at least he'd picked a place where he could see if some idiot stood up again. He knew it was the posse he was shooting at, because he could see the shadowy shapes of their horses moving around beneath the low hill.

And when that man stood up—the Brit, he was pretty certain—he'd taken his best shot. He didn't know whether the man was dead or not, but he comforted himself that he'd sure fallen hard enough to *be* dead.

But somebody else had been firing from that position, too. Somebody who had grabbed the sparking explosive out of the Brit's hand and tossed it far enough, but not so far that it did anybody any damage.

At least, he was pretty sure it hadn't.

More's the pity. If that shooter up there had known what was good for him, he'd have just let it blow him up. He'd suffer less that way. Less than what Rance planned to give him, anyhow.

Nobody was firing from the middle position right now, though, so Rance decided to change tactics. He'd go to the left first, he guessed. One side was as good as the other.

He began to creep, slowly, through the brush, his butt brushing his heels half the time. His chest had started hurting him again a while back, and the wound in his side was bothered some on account of all this crawling around.

In fact, it had opened up again.

At least the sun had gone down. During the day, whenever he slowed down to a walk or even a soft jog, his shirt was suddenly covered by flies, dining on the blood, he guessed. But there wasn't any sun, now, and the flies had all gone.

Course, that wouldn't keep some critter from smelling the blood and trying to seek him out.

He smiled. Well, he'd take care of that, if and when it happened. Once, when they were all kids, he'd gut shot a bear on purpose. He'd had a high old time following it around for two days while it died a slow and agonizing death.

Rafe and Rufus were pissed that he hadn't taken them along for the festivities.

They wouldn't miss the festivities this time, though. Not if he had anything to say about it.

"Go back and get my saddlebags, you fool," Amos hissed. He had protested mightily when Slocum moved him the last few feet—mainly, Slocum supposed, because he'd grabbed Amos's shot-up shoulder.

"It was the only way to get you around that bush," Slocum grumbled, then ducked just in time to miss a bullet flying overhead.

Amos made a face. "Will you please listen to me, Slocum? The saddlebags! I've got two more sticks of dynamite in the bloody things!"

Slocum, who had been holding Amos's head up, said, "Well, why the hell didn't you say so?" and let his head hit the ground.

He heard Amos's latent "Ouch! I hope this isn't going to be a habit!" as he crawled back toward the open, and the saddlebags.

Halfway there, he stopped. The gunfire had calmed down to a few occasional potshots, and he thought he heard something—or someone—crossing the brush beyond him. He froze and stared, gun in his hand and ready. He stayed there a full two minutes, and when no sound came again, no brush moved or rustled, he finally crept forward again.

Looney, that's where he was going. But he still needed to remind himself that somebody *was* out there. Someone unknown and very dangcrous.

That slug hadn't just ricocheted off thin air and turned around to hit Amos in the back.

• • •

Rance Carthage was in position once again. Slowly, he drew a bead on the back of the man on the left flank, waiting for the perfect opportunity.

The man rose up slightly.

Rance held his breath and squeezed the trigger, just as a lance of pain stabbed him in the goddamn shoulder.

The man he'd aimed at fell, but he was shot again, dammit! And by one of his own brothers' bullets—couldn't be anything else!

This time it was in the right shoulder, not the left, and when it struck him, he'd sat down hard. Cursing softly under his breath, he ripped the ruined fabric away from his shoulder and felt the bone grate as he moved.

In the joint! In the goddamn joint! No way he'd be able to get this one out by himself no matter how much whiskey he drank, no matter how many leather straps he bit down on. It was at the wrong angle, and it rendered his right arm next to useless.

Good thing he could still shoot with his left.

Not as well, of course, and he already had a wound that kept opening and closing at will in that arm. But it'd work good enough.

It had to.

Slocum, making his way back with the saddlebags, heard a strange absence of gunfire from his left. At first he thought that Arvil might be out of ammo, and coming back for more. Then, when he hadn't come by the time Slocum was back with Amos and digging out the dynamite, he figured something was wrong. Really wrong. It wasn't like Arvil to just quit.

But he didn't say anything to Amos. He let him supervise the bringing out of the dynamite, and listened while Amos strained to say, "That's a three-minute fuse, old chum. Or thereabouts."

"I know that," Slocum said as he pulled out a match and struck it on his heel.

"Oh yes, I forgot," Amos said, panting a little. "You know everything."

"That's right," Slocum said without looking at him. He lit the fuse, and they both watched it burn for a long minute and a half.

And then Slocum suddenly darted out into the clear, stood up and hurled that stick of dynamite as hard and as fast as he could toward the roof of the cabin, then dove back into the brush.

He and Amos both covered their ears.

Nothing happened.

Amos said, "I say, are you sure you didn't hit the water trough?"

"No, you blew that up already."

"Then what in the world—?"

The explosion took them both by surprise, and rolled Slocum off his heels.

It was immediately followed by a rain of burning

straw thatch and heated, flying rocks, one of which clipped Amos in the face before he had a chance to cover it with his arm.

They waited for the storm of debris to subside, and then Amos peeked out from behind his arm. "I believe you hit it, Slocum."

"Yup," Slocum said. "Stay here."

"As if you thought I could do anything else . . ." Amos muttered.

Slocum went out in the clear again, but stayed below the top of the hill. No one was shooting, now. Even Blue had stopped.

Slocum called, "Hello the cabin!"

No one answered.

He cocked his gun, took off his hat, and eased his head up over the rim of the hill.

The cabin was pretty much blown to hell. He guessed his throw had placed the dynamite square in the middle of the roof, and it had rolled nearly to the front before it went off. The roof was gone, and half the front wall was blown down. Small fires, set by flaming straw, blazed all around in the brush.

"I said, hello the cabin!" he repeated. "Rafe and Rufus Carthage, come out now if you're alive!"

From his right, he heard Blue holler, "Or even if you're goddamn dead!" and he smiled. It was good to know that Blue, at least, was in a fine fettle. He wasn't so sure about Arvil.

And they still had that sharpshooting lurker to deal with.

As if Blue was reading his mind, he called out, "Hey Arvil! You hear me?"

Silence.

"Think he's down, Blue," Slocum shouted. "He stopped firin' a bit ago."

"How's Amos?"

"He's down, but he ain't out," Slocum called back.

"Not by a long shot," Amos added loudly. And painfully by the sound of it.

"You got any more of that stuff?" Blue called.

"One more," Slocum replied.

"Well, toss it. I don't trust them boys to not be playin' possum on us."

Slocum grunted, then remembered himself and hollered, "Yup." And then he went back to where Amos waited with the last stick of dynamite.

19

When the third and last explosion blew the rest of the cabin apart, Rance Carthage was halfway back to his horses. As furious as he was, he knew his brothers—his baby brothers, his only kin—were dead. And he also knew that he couldn't take on the remaining two men with only half of one good arm.

Especially if one of those men was Slocum.

As much as it pained him, both spiritually—if such men can be said to have spirits—and physically, he made his way slowly to the horses.

Slowly was the only manner in which he could move, now. It seemed like that last slug he'd taken had awakened all the rest of the pains in his massive body. If he'd been closer to human, he would have just laid down and died. Or at last passed out.

But nobody had ever accused Rance Carthage of the least bit of humanity.

He reached the horses at last and somehow managed to get himself up on the sorrel. Slowly, to avoid sound as well as raising dust, he rode away from the cabin and what was left of his brothers and that sonofabitching, bastard posse at an angle, in the hopes that they wouldn't think to look out here for tracks.

Course, they probably would, but he might be in luck. The sky was clouding over, and there was barely enough moon to carefully ride by. Maybe the wind or the rain would come and wipe out his tracks.

Maybe, just once, for a change, something would be on his side.

Right now, he had to find somebody to take this slug out of his shoulder, and he thought he knew just where he could find someone.

Slocum rolled Amos over the top of the hill, against his protests, and then went looking for Blue. He met him halfway back, and unceremoniously pulled him down to the ground.

"Hey!" Blue shouted. "What'd you do that for?"

"Cause I think we got a sniper back there," Slocum hissed, tipping his head to the brush behind them. "Somebody shot Amos in the back."

Blue's face suddenly took a turn for the worse. "He ain't dead, is he?"

Slocum shook his head. "No. But I think Arvil is. Ain't heard a word or a noise from him since right after the first blast."

"Shit," Blue said sadly. "Sonofabitch. You wanna try and dig out this sniper a'yours?"

"Yup."

"All right," Blue said. Nothing could stop good old Blue. He added, "You fade out to the left, I'll take the right."

Slocum nodded, and disappeared into the brush. Blue did the same.

About twenty minutes later, after turning up nothing but a bent path through the weeds that led down to poor Arvil's body—also shot in the back, dead center—Blue whistled him up again.

Slocum made his way toward the sound of the bird trill, and there was Blue, standing fully upright in the shadows of the night.

"If he was here," Blue said, "he's gone now. Probably a ricochet, anyhow."

"Tell that to Arvil."

Blue's brows shot up. "In the back?"

Slocum nodded.

"Sonofabitch."

Slocum said, "If you're sure it's clear out here, I'll take your word for it. And I won't waste any time trackin' tonight."

"Yeah," Blue said, staring off toward the open range, into the night. "Looks like a blow's comin' up anyhow. Let's get back and take care'a Amos and bury those bodies. What's left of 'em, anyhow." He shook his head. "Jesus, I don't know what I'm gonna say to Harry and Dutch."

"Tell 'em Arvil died brave, helpin' to kill the last

of the Carthage boys," Slocum said. "That ought to do it."

But still, as they walked back toward Amos and the cabin, he wondered: Who the hell could have been out there, and what bone did he have to pick with Amos and Arvil?

Maybe he had a bone to pick with all of them.

Chances were, they'd hear from him again.

Right about the time that Rance Carthage's goal came into sight, just before the steady wind began to carry rain down to the thirsty ground, he fell off his horse.

He managed to hang onto his reins, but the bay moved off a few yards and started grazing.

Swearing a blue streak, he managed to get to his knees, then slowly, painfully pulled himself upright using the sorrel's saddle leather, hand over hand. He was too close to pass out now.

And too damned tough, he reminded himself bitterly.

The rain was pounding down now, but through it he could see the lights of the little shack. Maybe it was her, maybe she'd been thrown out and there was somebody else there, now.

It had better not be some land-grabber. He'd show them to take Letitia's shack away from her.

He walked slowly onward, leaning his bulk against the sorrel gelding, stumbling occasionally on the increasingly muddy soil. The bay simply followed along, grazing its way after them.

In front of the old shack, he pulled his right gun, the only usable one, now that his right shoulder was banged up, and knocked on the door.

He heard the sound of a rifle's cock, and then a female voice demanded, "Who is it, come to me out of this storm?"

"Letitia?" he asked, more relieved than he could have possibly imagined by the sound of her voice. "Tish, honey, it's Rance."

Suddenly the door swung open wide. A short women stood there, perhaps thirty or thirty-five, wearing a grubby dress. Her blond hair was knotted back in a tight bun, and her nails were black from working in the dirt all day. The look of joy on her face overcame her otherwise dull features.

She was the prettiest sight Rance had seen in a coon's age.

She took one look at his shirt, at the blood, and said, "Get in here right now and get the hell out of that shirt. I'll see to your horse."

"Horses," he corrected her.

Before he knew what hit him, she had kissed him square on the mouth, then he was inside, sitting on the edge of an Indian-blanketed bed, and she had closed the door between them.

•   •   •

The storm swept in full force before Slocum had a chance to get more than Arvil and one of the cabin's unfortunate former tenants underground. The third man, they blanketed and left until morning.

They couldn't find enough pieces of the Carthage boys to be worthy of a shovel full of dirt, and decided to leave the bits and pieces for the coyotes to pick.

There was enough of a wall left—the right rear corner—that the three of them could huddle in it against the wind, with their horses tethered nearby in the shelter of a couple of young cottonwoods.

Amos, who had been fixed up good and proper by Blue, lay against the wall with his blanket over his head—protection from the pelting rain—and said, "You know, you could have at least left us a little roof, Slocum."

"And I suppose you could'a done better?" Slocum asked. He was huddled beneath his blanket, too, as was Blue.

"Most certainly," Amos replied.

Blue was staring out at the rain. He said, "I don't believe we're gonna be able to track your sniper come morning, Slocum. Any tracks he left are wiped out by now."

"Yeah, I know," Slocum said. There was a tone of defeat in his voice. "Just wish I knew who the hell he was."

Blue nodded, and Amos said caustically, "Not half so much as so I."

Slocum snorted.

No matter how he turned it over in his head, he couldn't figure out who in the hell that sniper had been.

Now, he had made a lot of fellows mad at him over the years. Mad enough to shoot him in the back, if push came to shove. But he didn't figure that any of them could possibly be in this exact vicinity, or that they'd take down two other men when it was him they were after.

It was a puzzlement.

If he didn't know better, he would have sworn they hadn't killed Rance back in Hoopskirt.

He gave a disgusted shake to his head. No, that was pure impossible. He was reaching past the point of all reason.

It had to be somebody else.

"Hold still, blast your hide!" Letitia growled as she dug for the bullet. "Jesus Christ, if you ain't been shot up six ways from seven, Rance! Here, take another slug'a whiskey."

He lifted the bottle with his good left hand, and chugged down a few mouthfuls. "It hurts more comin' out than goin' in, Tish," he complained.

"That's cause it ain't gone nowhere yet," she said, taking the bottle from him and pouring another dose over her pocket knife. "I'm still tryin' to find the damned thing. Where was Rafe and Rufus when you got shot, anyhow?"

Rance stayed quiet on that, mulling over the right way to answer, when she leaned back, knife up in the air, and said, "Well?"

"They's dead, Tish. Murdered," he said at last.

She sat there, dumbly looking at him. Then she said, "No, really. Where was they?"

"Just told you," he growled.

Silence.

Then she seemed to gather herself. "You gonna get the sonsabitches that did it?"

"Soon's as you get me patched up."

She handed him a small knife scabbard. "Bite down on this."

He did, and she stuck the knife in his wound, twisted it twice, and flicked the offending slug across the room. It hit the wall, leaving a small, red speckle, then fell down between the worn floorboards.

20

Slocum didn't get much sleep that night.

He and Blue took turns keeping watch in case their sharpshooting friend came back, but even when it was Slocum's turn to sleep, he slept poorly. He couldn't blame it on the hard wet ground or the rocks that kept on digging into him, no matter how many he pulled from underneath him and chucked away. He'd been there, done that before.

He couldn't blame it on Amos, because they allowed him to sleep through the night, which he did like a goddamned baby.

He couldn't even blame it on the occasional—all right, more than occasional—thoughts that went through his head about the fair-haired and lovely Lucy, waiting for him back in Hoopskirt.

No, what kept him awake was the knowledge that somebody was out there. Somebody who was gunning for their whole party. Otherwise, why shoot Arvil and Amos? Why else bother to ride all the way out here, to the exact middle of nowhere?

At the break of dawn, they were up—well, he

and Blue were, anyway—burying the last of the bodies.

When they were finished, Blue and Slocum took off their hats and Blue did the honors. "Lord, we don't know who these two fellers were, but we ask you to take 'em into your arms along with Arvil Roman, who was one helluva cowhand and a real nice feller. Amen."

"Amen," echoed Slocum and put his hat back on.

"Amen and amen," came Amos's voice, through the craggy rock wall of what was left of the house. "Not going to say anything nice and uplifting about our friends, Rufus and Rafe, are we?"

Blue said, "I reckon the Lord'll put 'em where they belong without no comment from me," and folded his shovel away.

"True, so true," said Amos with a sigh. "Breakfast time. What I wouldn't give for some nice kippered herring . . ."

Slocum walked back over, and went to the fire they'd started before they commenced filling in the last grave. "You're gonna have to settle for coffee and cold fried chicken. How's the shoulder?"

"Better in one way," Amos admitted, "but bloody sore." He let out a theatrical sigh. "I fear it may be some time before I'm back to my old, devil-may-care self. I may find myself in need of a full-time nurse."

Slocum knelt down and poured out three cups of

coffee. "Like, for instance, Tipsy Magee?"

One-shouldered, Amos shrugged. "It had crossed my mind, Slocum, I must admit. I don't mind sharing if you don't."

"No, thanks," Slocum said, and handed up a cup to Blue, who had just entered the campsite. "I got somebody waitin' in Hoopskirt."

"Lucy?" asked Blue.

"Ah, yes," chimed in Amos. "I forgot, what with all the excitement. Nice of you to pick a stand-in, me having been wounded twice and all."

Blue snorted.

"Well, I was," Amos said as he accepted the next cup of coffee from Slocum. "Once in the side in your charming little hamlet, and again last night. I'm beginning to believe I have a bull's-eye painted somewhere on my person."

Mug in hand, Slocum sat down on the ruined cabin wall. He grinned, and just before he took a sip, he said, "Just be glad it's not lower, Amos."

Far away, at Letitia's shack, Rance Carthage wasn't feeling so hearty. In fact, he was having fever dreams something fierce. First he'd seen a Spanish dancer clicking her castanets and drumming her heels on his ceiling, and next, he'd seen Rufus sitting next to him, spoon-feeding him broth and telling him he was going to be all right, damm it.

During a brief period of lucidity, of which he had

few, he recognized Tish and asked, "Why's it so dad-blamed hot in here?"

"Cause you're burnin' up, darlin'," she'd replied matter-of-factly. "Your shoulder's gonna be fine, but what the hell did you take those other slugs out with? Small pox rags?" She sat down. "I sure hope you live. I wanna hear this story from beginnin' to end."

"Where's Cort?" he croaked, and she gave him a drink of water.

"Cort's gone, too," she said with no trace of emotion. "Drug to death by a green mule last spring. I shot the mule."

"Sorry," he said.

"No, you ain't," Letitia replied. "You ain't never been sorry for nothin' in your whole damn life, Rance Carthage. Not even killin' your own pa."

It was true. He hadn't felt bad. The old man had tried to make off with Rance's woman of the moment, and he deserved what he got.

"You ever tell your brothers about that?"

"Man's gotta keep some things to hisself, Tish," he muttered as the pictures began to come swimming back into his head.

At the foot of his bed, the old fishing hole up in Minnesota started to crystalize into view, and there was young Rufus, tossing in dynamite to get some easy bluegills and crappies for the pan.

"Rufus?" he shouted, there in the narrow cot.

"You be careful you dasn't blow off your hand, now, you damn fool!"

Vaguely, he was aware of somebody bathing his forehead with cool water, but in his fever dream he thought it was spray, spray from the dive that Rufus had just made into the lake to fetch those fish.

He smiled.

"Slocum, stop starin' at every hiding place we pass. He's long gone, I tell you," Blue insisted for the sixth time.

"Seems to me you ought to be a little more concerned, Blue," Slocum said grumpily. "After all, he could'a gone right just as well as left, and Arvil would'a been helpin' me toss dirt over you last night."

"But he didn't, did he?" Blue insisted. Blue had always been a relaxed sort of fellow, except for those cases when duty called loud and clear. He was just glad the sniper had taken off. If there were any repercussions, he'd deal with them when and if they happened.

Not Slocum, though. Oh, he was a real vinegar pot of activity, always thinking about something or other. If it wasn't women, then it was bad men with guns.

Blue wished Slocum would stick to the women-thinking side more. Things would be a lot quieter around the territory.

The whole of the West, come to think of it.

"My shoulder's doing quite nicely, in case anyone is even slightly interested," Amos said.

"We're not," Slocum and Blue said together.

"Fine," said Amos. "Perhaps, whilst we are blessed with a relative period of quiet, one of you will kindly tell me how you came to know each other?"

Slocum apparently didn't feel like talking, but Blue was up for some confab that had to do with something beside the Carthage boys or Slocum's damned sniper, so he started in.

"Was back in '72, wasn't it, Slocum?"

No answer. Oh well.

Blue continued, "I was a bounty hunter back then, and I was up in Montana, looking for a certain Elwood C. Candles. He'd stuck up three banks within a hundred miles, and folks was gettin' plumb annoyed."

Blue paused for effect, and Amos said, "Fascinating, old man. Do go on."

It didn't take much to encourage Blue. He said, "Well, it was the dead of winter and I was up in the high country—Montana's real cold when you get up high. I mean, you ain't met up with cold yet if you ain't spent a winter—"

"It was cold, Amos," Slocum broke in.

"So I gather," said Amos.

"All right," said Blue, who hated to have a good

story interrupted or thrown off track. But he persevered. "I was sneakin' up on old Elwood's cabin, see, sneakin' up through a snowbank on foot, just the top of my head peekin' over with a white hat on so's he wouldn't notice me comin', when all of a sudden old Slocum here—who's fifteen feet out front of me, and who I hadn't spied until that very moment, pops up and shouts, 'Elwood C. Candles, you're surrounded by sixteen special rangers. Come out now with your hands up, or we'll blast that cabin to hell and back!' "

Now, even Amos was listening intently, and with a big grin on his face. Blue figured he had a pretty damned good story going.

"So I just waited, you know, to see what would happen?" Blue went on. "And lo and behold, Elwood started firin' outta that place like hellfire itself was burning beneath him."

Amos laughed, but Slocum scowled. "C'mon, Blue," he said. "Get to the damned point."

"So, being back a little farther and havin' better cover, I went skitterin' round to the side of that cabin and opened up with everything I had," Blue said. "Both pistols blazin', like they say in the dime books, right through the side window."

Amos nodded eagerly.

"Anyhow, ol' Slocum took a couple of shots my way till he figured out what was goin' on, and then he started blastin with both sidearms, too. I'll be damned if we didn't sound like the whole cavalry was out there." Blue stopped to laugh and slap his thigh. "Hot damn, if that wasn't a funny sight. Pretty soon, Elwood hollers, 'I'm comin' out boys, you got me.' Pitches his guns out the front door, and follows them directly with his hands in the air."

"And that was how you met Slocum, was it?" Amos said with a grin.

"It sure was," Blue replied, still tickled with himself.

"Course, we had a fair amount of argument over the bounty," Slocum added.

"But it all got worked out," added Blue, somewhat hastily. "We run into each other a couple times since, but that was the first. Christ Almighty, I'm never gonna forget the look on Elwood's face when he seen there was only the two of us!"

"Where you goin' once we hit Hoopskirt, Amos?" Slocum asked, abruptly changing the subject.

"Crowfoot, first," Blue reminded him. "Gotta tell them cowardly folks that the territories are safe again. For a while."

He frowned and shook his head. He still couldn't believe that they'd scared up not one volunteer for the posse, not even after two people were killed.

"They don't rightly deserve to know, if you ask me," Slocum grumbled, obviously sharing Blue's feelings on the matter, "but I suppose you've gotta. Bein' a law man and all."

Blue nodded.

"Getting back to the point," Amos said dreamily, "I believe I'll head back to Armpit." He sighed, "Such a butt-ugly name for a town with such fabulously beautiful ladies . . ."

"Then back to Washington," Slocum added.

"Eventually." Amos winked.

"Nice to know that you boys got places to go," Blue said. "It's Hoopskirt for me, period. I've got a lot of ruffled feathers to soothe when I get back. Plus, I gotta scare up a new deputy till ol' Frank gets on his feet again."

Slocum said, "Seems to me you was already scrapin' the bottom of the barrel there, Blue."

Sadly, Blue nodded. "That I was, Slocum. That I was . . ."

They pulled into Crowfoot early that same evening, and nearly got themselves shot by one of the sentries the town council had belatedly seen fit to appoint.

Slocum grabbed the rifle away from the boy, once he got up close enough—and the sentry had realized his mistake—and tossed it in the nearest water trough.

"Look what you're shootin' at before you pull the trigger, boy!" he shouted.

The poor kid nearly wet his britches.

They rode on up to the livery, now vacant of either owner or equine boarder, and settled their own horses in, along with Arvil's mount, the pair the Carthage boys had stolen and the other two that had belonged to the original owners of the stone cabin.

Slocum figured maybe the sheriff could sell them and get the proceeds to those boys' next of kin, if they had any. There sure wasn't anything else of theirs left back there.

They went up to the sheriff's office, reported the deaths and were about to leave when Sheriff Coltrane said, "Wait just a minute, boys."

Slocum turned around. He hoped this was going to be quick. He wanted to get himself a hot bath and a shave in the worst possible way. And then he wanted to sleep for a day and a half, and then . . . well, then off to Hoopskirt and blond-headed Lucy and a few days of relaxation. And other things.

"After you come through here, after the . . . unpleasantness?"

"Yeah?" urged Slocum.

"There . . . there was somebody else came through," Coltrane continued nervously. "That's why I got guards posted all over town."

"Get to the point, man," Amos said offhandedly. "I'm in dire need of medical attention. Not to mention whiskey."

Slocum rolled his eyes, and Blue said, "What's the problem, Coltrane?"

21

Rance Carthage, Slocum thought furiously as he strode down to the saloon.

Goddamn that bastard, anyway!

Slocum had given up wondering just how the hell he'd survived that volley of slugs back in Hoopskirt. Some things just couldn't be explained by man nor God.

What he was wondering about at the moment was Rance's exact location.

He hadn't followed them back to Crowfoot. If he had, they all would have been dead, likely shot in the back. It was Rance's way, although he'd probably developed a few new and nasty habits since seeing his brothers blown to Kingdom Come.

"Sonofabitch," he hissed through clenched teeth as he pushed open the doors of the saloon.

"My sentiments, too," said Blue, who'd been dogging his footsteps down from the sheriff's office. They'd dropped a complaining Amos off at the doctor's office, just to make sure Blue had bandaged up his shoulder correctly.

"You know," Blue continued as they walked up

to the bar, "I don't get nothin' for this. Comes with the job. But whatever you're gettin' paid, it ain't enough, if you ask me."

It was only then that Slocum realized that he didn't know if he was getting paid anything at all. Now, this got him more annoyed than he already was, which was a good bit.

He should have thought to ask Amos, first thing. But he'd been so hot to get on the Carthages' trail . . .

"Whiskey," he said as he leaned an elbow on the bar. "Make it a double."

"Hell," said Blue. "Just bring the damned bottle." Then he turned back to Slocum. "You figure we need to post some more guards?"

Slocum snorted. "If that kid was a specimen of what they'd got to offer, I don't see that it'd do any good. Just pile up more bodies on the—what, five?— they've lost already."

Blue didn't say anything.

The bartender brought them a bottle and a couple of glasses, and they both gulped a shot. It tasted mighty good to Slocum, but he stopped with that and changed his next order to a beer. He wanted all his senses alert. There was no telling where Rance was or when he might just decide to show up.

Blue, on the other hand, poured himself out another whiskey. "Don't know about you, Slocum," he said, "but I need somethin' to set my nerves steady.

This 'first we're finished, then we're not' business is a little tough on a feller. Especially a feller who's main job for the past few years has been getting old ladies' cats down out of trees."

"Believe me," Slocum said, nodding, "I understand."

Turning around to lean against the bar, Slocum checked the place over while he sipped his beer. The place had only three customers, all of whom stopped whispering when he pivoted and tipped their hats to him.

Word traveled fast in these little towns, he guessed.

There looked to be only one whore available, but she wasn't exactly what Slocum was interested in. Even slightly. Aging, toothless, and wearing a tattered dress she sat at a back table all alone, playing solitaire and gumming a biscuit.

But then things began to look up. Through the rear door came a fresh little thing, dark-haired and pretty. She was carrying a box of groceries.

Well, crud. Maybe she was only the delivery girl.

But he kept an eye on her, just the same.

She carried her box to the edge of the bar, saying, "Here you go, Ike."

Then Ike, the bartender whispered something to her and tipped his head in the direction of Blue and Slocum. She looked down their way and smiled.

Slocum tipped his hat. Blue, being busy staring at his whiskey bottle, didn't notice.

The girl made her way down the narrow barroom and sidled up next to him. This time, Blue noticed, since the target of her sidle was right between the two of them.

"I hear you two got the Carthage boys," she said, right out. "We're grateful, sirs."

"It was three of us," Blue broke in. "Well, four, actually. Old Arvil didn't make it, God rest him, and Amos is up at the doc's."

"I reckon you heard about our other troubles," she said, directly to Slocum and ignoring Blue entirely.

"Yeah," Slocum said. Behind the girl's back, Blue tipped his hat and turned back to his whiskey. "We heard."

"You're the one they call Slocum, ain't you?" she asked, batting her dark lashes just a tad.

"Yup," he replied, and gave her a smile. "How'd you know that?"

Her fingers trailed down his arm. "Oh, word gets around. You know."

He sure did. And right at the moment, he'd forgotten all about Lucy and Hoopskirt. He asked, "You got a few free minutes?"

She smiled seductively. "Oh, I got more than that, Slocum. A lot more."

He drained his beer quickly, and as he walked

toward the stairs with her, Blue called, "Just come
runnin' if you hear gunshots, ol' buddy!"

"You got it," replied Slocum, then turned to the
girl again. "What'd you say your name was,
honey?"

Hands propped on her hips, Letitia shook her head.
"I swear, Rance Carthage, I ain't never in my life
seen a man for healin' like you."

His fever was down to a tolerable level, and he
was sitting up in bed, spooning at a bowl of broth
Tish had made up for him. It wasn't bad, considering it was made with snake meat.

"I'm hard to kill, Tish," he said. "All us Carthages are. Took a couple-three blasts of dynamite to
take out Rafe and Rufus." He said this with some
anguish, but a larger degree of pride.

"They were a couple of jackasses," he added,
"but they went out like goddamn Carthages."

"Well," she said, sitting down, "that's all a body
can ask, ain't it?"

"Reckon." He handed his empty soup bowl over.
"Got anythin' a man can chew on?"

"Seein' as how you done so good with the broth,
I reckon I can rustle some up," she said. She got up
and started messing about in the kitchen, which was
merely the other side of the lean-to. "Suppose you'll
be off before long."

"Yup," he said, pulling himself up a little higher

in the bed. It wasn't any too comfortable, but it beat a bed of rocks and dirt out under the stars.

"Don't suppose you'll be back, then," she added, without looking at him.

He knew that tone. He'd known Letitia since they were both kids, but that didn't keep him from reading that "my man's gone now, so why don't you take his place?" question in her voice, even if it was unspoken.

He said, "Might. Might not. Depends."

"Depends on what?" she asked, trying to keep her voice casual. But the attempt was fruitless against Rance.

"Depends on a lotta things," he said, ending the discussion. For now. "What you makin' me to eat, anyhow?"

The girl's name, oddly enough, was Honey, and she had been home with a sick sister the day the Carthage boys rode into town, killing little Penny and the stable owner on their way through.

She had come back in time for the third man to enter town, though, and she had been among those who chased him from the saloon.

"I threw tomatoes," she said proudly. "That's what I was restockin' from Gowdy's general store."

"You get many orders for tomatoes in a bar?" Slocum asked as he slipped off her dress.

"You'd be surprised," she replied and, with that, went to work on his belt buckle.

He hadn't realized how much he needed the comfort and release of a woman, and he took her across the table, sweeping the contents of its cloth aside and laying her, spread-eagled, across its surface.

Standing at the edge, between her legs, he hooked her heels behind his neck. He ran one big palm over her full breasts and flat belly and then, with one quick thrust, drove into her.

She let out a sound, halfway between pleasure and surprise, but Slocum paid it no mind. He wanted—no, needed—the release of an orgasm now, and he single-mindedly pumped her. First fast, then slow, then fast again, until he felt himself rising up, felt that tickle in his loins grow into a bonfire, then a conflagration.

Then he came in a sudden, spurting flood that drained him of the past days of stress and turmoil and too many dead bodies. He was vaguely aware that she came, too, that she made a tiny strangled scream in the back of her throat.

When he opened his eyes and looked down, her eyes were half-lidded and she was panting hard, her mouth open a little. A thin skin of sweat coated her brow, and her hair was damp at the temples. The cords at the sides of her neck were just beginning to relax.

To Slocum, she looked prettier now than ever before.

He lay his hand on her belly, rubbing it in soft circles as he felt her inner thrumming carry through him, through his slowly wilting cock. Which was about to get hard again.

"My goodness," she breathed. "I may have to pay *you!*"

He smiled. "That was just to get me loosened up, Honey," he said, and chuckled when her eyes opened all the way and grew round. "What do you say that you and me wander on over to your bed?"

Slowly, sinuously, she sat up, still impaled, and hugged him close. "I'd admire it," she whispered into his ear, just before she kissed him.

Fully dressed and sitting on the edge of the lumpy bed, Rance Carthage stormed, "You let me out of here, woman!"

One more *no* out of her and, childhood friend or not, third cousin or not, he'd wring her neck.

But she said, "Not on your life, Rance," and he still couldn't bring himself to kill her. And he couldn't exactly figure out why.

"You listen to me, Rance Carthage," she went on, arms crossed, feet sct, brow creased. "First off, its nighttime, and the moon's clouded over. You wouldn't be able to see where the hell you was goin', and you wouldn't get twenty feet a'fore your horse'd step in a hole and break a leg. Second, them poultices ain't finished their work yet, and you ain't leavin' until they have. And that's gonna be at least morning. And third," she added, softening her tone, "I want you should stop over in the breeding shed, iffen you get my drift."

Now, this didn't come exactly as a surprise to Rance, who figured Tish was after him to replace her dead, muledrug husband, but he hadn't expected her to be quite so . . . blatant about it.

But he said, "I get your drift, Tish." And he felt himself swelling in his pants already.

He waited a moment, just to make sure that someone wasn't fooling him, and then he said, "So when you want to do it?"

"Now's as good a time as any, I reckon," she said, and walked the few steps to the side of the bed. "Now, take off them britches you just put back on."

"All right," he growled, pretending to be grumpy. He knew no other way. "But you get your ass outta them work skirts. I likes to see what I'm diddlin'."

He looked down, clumsily unfastening his buttons, then looked up. "And bare your titties, too," he said. "I like titties. I wanna see what kind you growed up to have."

22

Blue was pretty well in his cups and had switched over to black coffee, with a side of raw, sliced tomatoes, when Amos strolled into the bar.

Amos, who had spent more than enough time with the doctor, so far as he was concerned, was wearing a fresh shirt, one shoulder and one side of which were fat with the clean bandages that lay beneath.

"So what'd he say?" was the first thing out of Blue's mouth. It came out a little slurry.

"That you did a fine job of patching, and that I shall live to ride another day," Amos said. He sat down and signaled the barkeep for a beer. "And you, old friend?"

"Aw, hell," Blue said. "I got myself too sozzled. Tryin' to undo it now." He cut off a slice of tomato, slathered it with sugar, and swallowed it whole. "Thinkin' about what Rance Carthage might'a done to my folks back home. You know, once he realized he was alive and all."

Amos nodded. He supposed he'd be drunk, too,

if he were in Blue's boots. At least he had the sense
to stop when he had.

Amos said, "Where's Slocum?"

Blue rolled his eyes toward the ceiling. "Where
else? You don't suppose he just went through the
place, killin' everybody, do you?"

"Who? Slocum?"

Blue sighed. "No, Rance. I'd hate for anything
else to happen to them people. They got nobody
there to protect 'em, 'cept Frank. And he's stove up.
Course, he's useless when he's fine, too, but at least
he was a body."

Amos nodded sympathetically, and reached for
the pot on the table. He refilled Blue's cup. "Here,
my friend. Have another."

Actually, it sounded like Slocum had the right
idea, but the only other soiled dove in the place—
that he could see, anyway—was a sad-looking
woman at the corner table. She clenched a bent cig-
arette between lips which hid no teeth.

Sad, so sad. You'd think they'd take up a collec-
tion or something. After all, a soiled dove's appearance said a great deal about the quality of the town
in which she chose to work.

He hoped Slocum had ended up with better.

Slocum lay back against the pillows, enjoying
Honey's breasts, with which he toyed idly, and a
pretty nice cigar. Not a Havana—or at least, not an

expensive one—but certainly passable. After the last few days, it was practically heaven.

Especially after three helpings of Honey, he thought to himself, smiling. She wasn't only a pretty little thing, she was a pretty fair piece of ass.

Right now, he'd worn her out and she was sleeping, curled up at his side, naked as the day she was born, and smiling softly in her sleep.

He hoped she'd continue to have reason to smile.

He didn't expect Rance to come riding into Crowfoot tonight. It was too dark. There wasn't enough moon showing.

But wherever he'd got to, he'd be pretty damned sure to come riding in tomorrow.

Slocum figured that maybe he'd got hurt again, or else those wounds he'd suffered back in Hoopskirt had finally caught up with him. And like an animal, he'd probably gone somewhere to hole up until he felt better. At least, until he felt like he could kill again.

For Rance, that wouldn't have to be much of an improvement. That snake would likely shoot somebody from the grave, if he had to.

So things must have been pretty bad for him to take off last night. Slocum hoped that things had been bad enough that he'd died. But he doubted it.

If he was going to be ready for whatever came tomorrow, he supposed he'd best get some shut-eye.

He stubbed out his cigar, blew out the light, cuddled up with Honey, and closed his eyes.

Since the town of Crowfoot had no hotel, both Blue and Amos slept in the saloon—Amos atop the planks that served as the bar top, and Blue across one of the larger tables. His legs dangled off the edge and his boots rested precariously on a chair's back.

The toothless whore, taking pity on them, had asked them both upstairs to share her bed, but for some reason, they'd refused politely. Sighing, she went on upstairs, alone.

Sheriff Coltrane dropped by in time to witness her asking them, and wasn't surprised when they refused. Of course they refused to acknowledge his presence, too. Well, maybe they didn't notice him. After all, he was standing outside the door, on the walk, and they were pretty tired.

He hadn't gone in. Neither had he offered them the comfort of his home, such as it was. He'd let them stretch out on the hard wood and go to sleep, and he had gone on with his rounds.

It was best to keep things as normal as possible, wasn't it? That's what he thought, anyway. He'd heard Sheriff Blue Parker tell him that the most exciting things, up in Hoopskirt, were righting the outhouses again after the kids dumped them on their sides on All Hallow's Eve.

Well, that was about the extent of his hardest duty, too. Except he didn't have what he suspected was Blue's background. He was a small rancher, pure and simple, who had accepted this job because it added thirty bucks a month to his already meager income. A rancher who only ran forty head of cattle didn't tend to make much money.

He never imagined anything like these goddamn Carthage brothers even existed when he signed on. They weren't worth thirty lousy dollars a month. Nothing was worth that.

All right, Slocum and the others had killed two of them. But according to Slocum, that man who'd killed Tom Dixon, Phil Grady and Charlie Estaban right out there on the street yesterday had been the third brother. One they thought they'd already killed.

Now they said that he'd likely be back again, and who was to say the first two wouldn't show up, too? It was just plain too much to even think about. Hell, poor little Penny Springer's daddy was still sedated over at the boarding house.

A shiver went through Coltrane, unbidden.

It didn't just make him mad. It scared the hell out of him.

He stopped down at the livery to identify the horses the Carthage boys had taken. He supposed they belonged to the livery, all right. The other two mounts came as something of a surprise. He knew they belonged to Chris and Gene Hutchins.

He'd known Chris and Gene. He'd stood up at Chris's wedding.

It crossed his mind that for the first time, he was glad that Chris's Ella was gone to Jesus these last five years. He'd sure hate to be the one to tell her that Chris had been murdered.

Coltrane checked in with his sentries, such as they were, then slowly, thoughtfully, walked back up to the jail.

By the time he got there, he'd made up his mind.

He left his badge on the desk, went out back and saddled his horse. It would be very slow going tonight, but at least it would be going.

He didn't much care where.

And then, as an afterthought, he went back inside and left a single sheet of paper under his badge. And on the paper, he wrote, "I'm sorry. I quit."

Rance Carthage snuck out of bed before dawn, leaving a snoring Tish to hog the covers. She'd been all right last night, but man, she was sure ugly in the morning.

He didn't figure he'd be back.

Ever.

Well, unless he got shot up again, and just happened to be in the vicinity.

He let himself out, and by the first rays of the early morning sun, saddled the bay. He was about to take the sorrel, too, when he thought better of it. Best leave Tish something that she could either ride or eat—sort of placate her, like—in case he ever did find himself in need of her again.

Satisfied, he loaded up the bay with the rest of his gear and took off at jog, cutting across country and making a beeline for Crowfoot. He'd bet anything those brother-killing bastards were holed up there. And if they were, he was going to teach them—and that goddamn tomato-tossing town—a lesson they'd never forget, not in a million years.

By Christ, he was going to teach them good!

Slocum woke to the loud *bang, bang, bang* of somebody pounding on his door, and it took him a few seconds to realize where he was, and why. And with whom.

He climbed over the just-waking Honey and, wrapping a sheet around himself, yelled, "Who the hell is it?"

"Blue!" came the familiar voice. "We got a little problem."

"So what else is new?" Slocum muttered to himself, then called back, "Be out in a minute."

With a dejected Honey swinging her legs back and forth off the side of the bed, Slocum hurriedly dressed and strapped on his gun belts. He gave her a quick kiss good-bye, dropped a few dollars on the dresser, and started to go out the door.

"Don't pay me," she said softly.

He turned. "Huh?"

"Just . . . just don't pay me, that's all." She was looking down at the floor.

Slocum scooped up the coins and put them back in his pocket. He'd buy something pretty for her, that's what he'd do. If he lived through Rance.

"All right, Honey," he said softly. "But you're gonna get a little present if we make it through this."

She didn't answer, but then, he didn't wait for one. He was out the door and down the hall before she would have had time to open her mouth.

Blue was waiting at the end of it, leaning back against the wall, his hat cocked forward.

"What now?" asked Slocum.

"Sheriff Coltrane quit in the middle of the night," Blue said, slowly standing erect. "Took everything but his badge and the keys to the cell."

"Can't see that he was doin' us much good, anyhow," Slocum replied as he started down the stairs.

Blue followed him downward. "Except for one thing," he said. "He's the feller what got all these so-called sentries organized. They was pretty lousy, but they was better than nothin' at all. Most of 'em went home and pulled the covers over their heads—maybe climbed clear under their beds, for all I know—the second they heard he was gone."

"Great," said Slocum in disgust, and without thinking, put his fist right through the plastered wall. "Just great. Ouch."

23

Rance Carthage came within two miles of Crowfoot just before noon. He knew he was on the right path, because he'd joined up with the posse's tracks about six miles back.

Three riders, leading a passel of unmounted horses.

Wasn't it bad enough that they'd had to blow his poor little brothers to hell without taking their horses, too?

Christ on a sonofabitching crutch!

He reined in his horse and sat there, thinking. What to do? Go after the posse first, or shoot up that little shithole of a town?

Course, maybe the posse was still in the town. He hadn't thought of that before, and the idea brightened him up some. He could kill two birds with one stone, so to speak.

But he'd best be careful. These boys were damn tricky.

Finally, he reined his horse to the east and began to make a wide circle around Crowfoot. He knew they'd be headed back to Hoopskirt if they had, in fact, left Crowfoot. If he had a choice to make, he could make it then.

Slocum had been busy.

First, he and Blue and Amos had gone door to door, rousting out every able-bodied man they could pry away from his wife's apron strings, armed him with plenty of ammo, and situated him on the roofs or upper porches of the buildings all around the town.

Strangely enough, the women seemed more riled than the men. They had several female volunteers, which they gladly accepted.

"How's your shoulder, Amos?" Slocum asked, after they'd dragged their thirteenth or fourteenth volunteer into place.

"Lovely, thank you, just lovely," Amos replied through clenched teeth. "It only pains me when I move."

But he kept on moving, God bless him, and Blue did just as much, if not more. By noon, they were all set up, and the few women who hadn't exactly volunteered for rooftop duty were scurrying around the town, carrying baskets of sandwiches and lime-ade.

"How odd," said Amos, eyeing a ham sandwich. He and Slocum were up on top of the bank, looking out toward the western hills. "I don't believe I've ever been on a catered stakeout before."

"Shut up and drink your limeade," Slocum grumbled around a mouthful of sandwich. He'd gotten chicken, and it was as dry as hell. Not enough salt, either.

Also, more than half the day had gone by, and there was still no sign of Rance. He didn't know quite what to think of that. Maybe old Rance had crawled into a hole somewhere and died.

Now, there was a happy thought, but Slocum knew better than to count on it. He just didn't have that kind of luck.

By two o'clock, there was still nothing, and the men were beginning to get grumbly. Several of them had tried to leave their posts only to be forced back up, at gunpoint, by Blue or Amos.

By three, the heat on the rooftops was getting to all of them, Slocum included. He let the men on the roofs go down into the saloon, by shifts, for twenty minute intervals. A few tried to scurry home, but either Blue or Amos was always there with a shotgun and a scowl. Or, in Amos's case, a smile.

Slocum came down from the bank roof exactly three times, to patrol the streets. The place looked as empty as a starving coyote's gut.

At four o'clock, it finally dawned on him that Rance, if he was out there, was likely waiting for sundown. He would, if he were in Rance's place.

He'd be able to get in closer without being seen, be able to move around in the shadows.

Well, this lookout time hadn't been wasted. The men had at least got the feeling that they were protecting their town. They had banded together, even if it was sort of against their collective will.

He couldn't wait to tell them that their duty wouldn't end at sundown.

Well, hell. Amos had gotten him into this. Let Amos tell them. And while he was at it, Slocum reminded himself to ask Amos about any pay that might be coming his way.

It had better be, or he and Amos were going to have some words, by God.

By just before sundown, Rance Carthage was west of town, in the low hills that hugged the horizon. His horse was tethered down below him, and he was on his belly with his binoculars to his eyes, watching the town.

He'd about got the pattern figured out by now: when the men on certain buildings went down for a break or to take a leak, and when they came up again.

His wounds were bothering him a little bit, but he'd remembered to change the poultice, like Tish had told him the night before. The old ones had come away filled with pus and the new ones stung when he put then on, but he figured that the pain was a sign of healing.

Just on the off chance that anybody was trying to follow him, he'd buried the old bandages two feet down, beneath a palo verde.

He was glad to get rid of the pus, too. Felt about fifteen pounds lighter with it gone.

Good old Tish. He was feeling a little bad about riding off on her like that.

But not that bad.

Through the glasses, he watched as a tiny, antlike dot of a man climbed down from a roof near the center of town, then disappeared into an alley, while another ant-man emerged from another alley and began to climb up to another of the town's many flat roofs.

That was one good thing about adobe. You couldn't build a pitched roof on it to save your life. It made watching for men a whole lot easier.

He glanced back over at the sun, which was sinking into the west. About another half-hour, he figured, and he could get ready to go on down. If he traveled slow, he could make it near to town before he came into sight. Further, if he left the horse staked out and went in on foot.

He'd been awful glad to see that the posse hadn't left town. There was no sign of tracks going out the other way, toward Hoopskirt.

The fools. They were about to meet their maker, sure as shooting.

And he knew. He was going to be the one pulling the trigger.

Rance began his trek down to Crowfoot a little later, when the sky had gone to purples and oranges. He knew they couldn't see him from the town, even with spyglasses, at this distance because of the darkness.

And so he took his time, ambling along, resting his wounded body for the trials he'd be putting it through later on.

Although he didn't think of the ensuing conflict as a trial. He just thought of it as revenge.

He hoped his brothers were watching from somewhere, wherever they were now. He wanted them to know that he was alive, and he was getting even for them. And once he got even, he planned to have a good enough time for all three of them.

Oh, there'd be hangings and rapes and heads on spikes; bodies ripped apart by horses, arms and legs chopped off, and all manner of fun. Old Rafe and Rufus would have really gotten a kick out of what he had planned for the citizens of Crowfoot.

And never did he entertain, for one solitary moment, a single, simple doubt that he was not perfectly able to do it.

Not once.

• • •

Once the sun began to set, Slocum himself went around to all the posts, speaking softly with the men, reassuring them, but giving them little doubt that they'd better hold their positions and keep their eyes open, or else.

He left it up to them to figure out the "or else" part.

By the looks on their faces, most of them seemed to be doing a pretty fair job of it.

Once they'd made their final rounds with supper, he and Amos—who had a much more persuasive way with women, at least en masse—rounded up all those females who hadn't taken up guns and posts, and all the town's children, and put them in the bank. It was the sturdiest building in town, Slocum figured, and the easiest to defend.

One matron, angry about everything from the assaults on her town to the indignity of being made to hide in a bank, said, "What kind of men are you? You say there's only one of them out there! Why, we chased him out of town with eggs and tomatoes!"

Slocum started to growl something rude, but fortunately Amos cut him off. "Because, my dear madam," he said. "This one man is worth fifteen others. I, myself, have seen him single-handedly kill thirteen woman and children in the space of three minutes, and all without a backward glance. I assure you, he is quite ruthless."

That speech, delivered in Amos's patented cool-but-in-charge tone, shut her up pretty quick.

"Thirteen women and children in the space of three minutes?" Slocum asked as they climbed up to the roof.

"A slight exaggeration," Amos admitted. "But it worked, didn't it?"

Night had fallen by this time. Slocum said, in a low voice, "Y'know, I did think about lightin' fires all around the town. The place is small enough that we could'a done it."

Amos nodded. "Once again, you've read my mind. I decided against it because I figured it would only slow him down. Keep him out until we ran out of kindling, so to speak."

Slocum scowled. "Get out of my head, Amos."

Amos snorted a laugh, then asked, "Where's Blue?"

"Makin' rounds. He figured that since Crowfoot didn't have a sheriff anymore, if was up to him to see things were locked up proper."

Amos shook his head. "As if it matters a whit."

"It does to Blue," Slocum said, and lay down on his belly, resting his rifle on the rim of the roof's edge.

"Sheriff," said Amos. "I keep forgetting."

Slocum turned on his side, "Speakin' of forgettin', did you forget to tell me just how much this little job of yours pays?"

Amos cocked a brow. "Why, you mean to tell me that you wouldn't do it for the Queen—I mean, President—and country?"

"I don't see him out here helpin' us none," Slocum replied dryly.

Amos tipped his head. "Point well taken, Slocum. Well, the truth of the matter is that—"

"Slocum!" shouted a voice from several rooftops over. "I think I seen somethin'! Over there!"

"So much for the element of surprise," Amos muttered as Slocum took out his spyglass and held it to his eye. "You see anything?"

After a moment, Slocum said, "Just black. And a pair of coyote eyes flashin'."

Amos called back, in a stage whisper, "All clear. It was only a coyote. Good watching, Fred."

"You're gonna compliment him on that?" Slocum grumbled.

"Better that than he goes to sleep," Amos replied. "I'm going over to the other side of the roof, now. I trust you won't be too lonely."

Slocum didn't turn to look at him. "Aw," he growled, "get out of here, Amos."

24

Rance stopped his horse about a mile and a half from town and sat there, in the saddle, thinking things over. He'd changed his bandages a second time, and there wasn't as much pus, but it was still flowing strong. He felt a little feverish, too.

But then, that could be marked up to the excitement of the battle ahead, the thrill of the rising body count and seeing the two men who had put him in prison once before dying—slowly—before his eyes.

Still, he dismounted, took off his shirt, and laboriously changed his poultices and bandages one last time. He figured there would be a doctor's office. He could steal any further supplies he might need.

After all, the town would be his.

The last bandage tied and the old ones buried, he put on his shirt again—now a faint pink, after Tish's scrubbing—and checked his pocket watch.

Eight twenty-five.

He wondered if they were growing weary of waiting for him to show up. Had they gone home to their wives and their suppers and their porches? Did they think Rance Carthage was dead? Or worse, had run away?

Fat chance. Not in a million years.

He led his horse another hundred yards or so, then decided it was time. Pulling down his rifle and his bands of extra ammunition, slinging one over each shoulder—wincing when one hit his right shoulder at the wrong angle—along with his extra canteen and a few other items, he shooed away the horse. It walked ten feet, then started to graze. It would be no problem.

This was a good thing, because now wasn't the time to waste a bullet on it. He was too close. It would be heard.

He raised his binoculars to his eyes for the third time in as many hours, and scanned the darkened rooftops. Nothing. Nothing.

But there! There was a head!

So they had not abandoned their posts after all.

He smiled. It pleased him that they must be very afraid.

As well they should be. Death was coming, and its name was Rance Carthage.

Sheriff Coltrane had thought better of his actions at about two that afternoon.

What had brought him to this realization—that he should go back and do what he was hired to do— was his discovery of the bodies of two men, left to rot on the open plain between Crowfoot and Hoop-skirt.

They weren't so far gone that he didn't recognize them, though. They were the two fellows who had ridden into town with Slocum and Sheriff Parker and the rest. The two who had decided to turn back.

Dutch and Harry, that was it, wasn't it?

He'd buried them right there, of course. A couple of days in the heat didn't go very far in helping a body hang together, especially when you had to transport it over the back of a horse.

He'd made the men crosses out of some ironwood limbs he found, and piled the rocks high on their cairns to keep the coyotes out.

And then, at about six, he'd turned back.

It was either the best or the worst decision he'd ever made in his life.

At about eight-thirty, he saw, in the gloom up ahead, something moving. Something too big to be a coyote.

He had a spyglass in his saddlebags, and he pulled it out and had a look through it, but it didn't do much good. It was too dark, and the rider—at least he'd established that part—was too far off.

Now, the first thought that came into his head was that it was Rance Carthage. But the second, charging hard on the heels of the first, was the question about why in the hell Carthage would be coming from the west.

That didn't make any sense at all. He should have been coming from the south. And shouldn't he already be in town, if he was coming at all?

"You're givin' yourself a case of the collywobbles, Coltrane," he muttered. "Cut it out."

And then the rider disappeared.

Coltrane checked through the glass again, but there was nothing. Of course, the brush was so high out here, in places, that if the rider had dismounted and let his horse graze, it was possible that nothing would stick up into viewing range.

Still . . . could he have imagined it?

Cotrane sat on his horse, holding very still. In truth, he was heartily tempted to just turn around and go back the way he'd come. He'd been looking for a good excuse ever since he'd buried those bodies and decided to do the "right" thing.

He didn't want to do it, though, that was for certain.

But after a moment, he reined his horse off to the side, avoiding the possibly imaginary rider's path, and headed toward town at a walk.

Christ, it was blacker than the devil's innards out here!

At a quarter to nine, Amos, who was on the northwest corner of the bank roof, whispered, "Slocum! Rider coming in."

Quickly, Slocum scrambled over to his position,

and grabbed away his spyglass, asking, "It Rance?"

"No," said Amos, at the same time Slocum brought up the glass and squinted through it.

It wasn't Rance. The figure was far too thin, not muscle-bound in the slightest. Rance Carthage's massive arms would bow out wider than his horse's belly.

"Who the hell is it, you think?" Slocum said, handing the glass back.

Amos shrugged. "I might be mistaken, but I believe Crowfoot's sheriff has had a change of heart."

"Great," Slocum grunted. "That's all we need. Coltrane messin' things up."

"Seems to me we should be glad of the help," Amos said, a lot more calmly than Slocum felt at the moment. "Any help, no matter from what quarter."

"Fine," was all Slocum said, then made his way, on hands and knees, back to his previous position and settled back in.

He heard Amos say, across the space of the alley below, "Coltrane's coming in from the northwest," to the man on the next roof. "Pass it along."

It took exactly seven minutes for the news to make it around town and circle back to Slocum. "Don't shoot to the northwest, Slocum," called a voice softly. "It's Sheriff Coltrane."

"Yeah, yeah," grumbled Slocum. He kept his eyes peeled, out into the distance.

•   •   •

At nine thirty-three, Rance Carthage was secreted in the bushes at the edge of town, right behind Chambers Feed and Grain. He was right beneath the ladder that led up to the roof, as a matter of fact.

The lookout posted up there should be coming down at any time, because, if they were going in the circular pattern he thought they were, it was his turn next. The man on the roof next to him had just gone back up.

Rance had held very still. The man didn't see him in the darkness.

Sure enough, after five long minutes, he saw a shadowy shape, then heard footsteps above, on the ladder. He bided his time, waiting until the dark blob turned into a shape with legs that came down nearer and nearer until boots, then calves, then thighs were even with his head.

Still, he waited until the man stepped down to the ground before he lunged, grabbed him, and snapped his neck in one smooth motion.

Once he established that the dead man had no weapons that were better than those Rance already had, he quietly dragged the body—a middle-aged fellow, looked like a storekeeper—back into the bushes.

Then he, himself, climbed up the ladder.

He was halfway up when a voice whispered, "Frank? That you? You forget somethin'?"

Rance paused. "Yeah," he whispered, then continued on up, his gun drawn and ready. He didn't want to start shooting this early in the game, but if that was the way it had to be, so be it.

But when he got up to the rooftop, the other man up top was staring out toward the desert, away from him, and was clear down at the other end of the building to boot.

Easy pickings.

Handling his bulk as gracefully as a dancer, Rance moved softly down the roof, creeping up behind the other lookout. He had to be a kid. Couldn't be more than fifteen.

Well, say good-bye to ever seein' sixteen, Rance thought just as the boy turned around, eyes popping in surprise.

Before the kid could call out, Rance had one big hand over his mouth and the other at the back of his head. He twisted.

Snap!

He let the boy's body down slowly, to avoid making any sound, then sat down next to it.

The kid had a spyglass, a box of shells, and a shotgun. A knife, too, likely his papa's second-best pocket whittler. Rance already had himself twelve inches of Arkansas toothpick, and so laid the boy's knife aside disdainfully.

With a grunt, he shook his head. Like they thought these toys would be enough to hold him off!

Him, Rance Carthage, whose brothers had just been murdered in a foul and cowardly manner!

It never crossed Rance's mind that he had ever done anything wrong, not really, not in his entire life. He couldn't figure out why anyone would be angry with him just for having a good time. Neither did he give a good goddamn how they felt.

He had no sense of right or wrong in him. But if he had anything human in him at all, it was a strong sense of brotherhood.

And that had been taken from him.

He picked up the spyglass and began slowly scouting up and down the street. If those bastards who had shot him, put him in prison and killed his brothers were up here, he'd find out quick enough.

He peered up and down the road, then up and down the rows of rooftops, but all he could see was an occasional hatted head sticking up here or there.

And then he saw something more interesting. Someone riding right down the middle of the road, from the opposite end of town.

He smiled. Well, somebody sure had him some balls, didn't he?

The funny thing was that Rance's wounds hadn't bothered him one whit since he got off his horse and started this final walk to town. He supposed the poultices had something to do with it, but it was more likely the thrill of the hunt. He was going to have himself a mighty good time, and he knew it.

Quietly, he stepped over the boy's body and made his way to the ladder. Down he went, moving carefully so as not to make the boards creak, and then he moved north, hugging the buildings, in the direction of the rider.

He'd teach whoever that was to be cocky about Rance Carthage!

Sheriff Coltrane was welcomed with loud whispers of, "Good to see you," and "Howdy, Sheriff," and the occasional, "Stinkin' coward!" as he rode up the deserted street.

When he got to the bank, Blue leaned over the edge of the roof and hissed, "Psst! Sheriff Coltrane! Glad to have you back!"

"That you, Blue?"

"Yeah, and Slocum and Amos are up here with me. We got somebody on every roof in town."

Coltrane got off his horse and started toward the outside steps, but before he made it three feet, Blue whispered once more, "No, inside. We got all the women and kids in the bank and we need somebody to . . . guard 'em."

It was what he should have expected, Coltrane thought. He'd girded his loins and come riding back in with his tail betwixt his legs, and now he was the official baby-sitter for the town, goddamm it.

With mixed emotions, he signaled Blue that he'd heard, then started back toward the bank's entrance.

He was nearly to the door when somebody else, somebody in the alley, hissed, "Psst! Over here!"

"Who is that?" he called softly. He didn't know why the hell everybody in town was whispering, but he supposed they had their reasons.

"Help!" whispered the voice.

Automatically, he started toward it, toward the alley. He was the sheriff, after all. Maybe somebody was hurt. He'd have to find the doc, he supposed, and then he wondered where the doc was tonight.

"What's wrong?" he asked as he turned the corner, into the mouth of the alley. It was as dark as Kentucky dirt back there.

Squinting, he took a step in.

Suddenly a hand lashed out and, with more power than Coltrane could have ever imagined, grabbed him around the mouth and hauled him back. There was a flash of steel, huge, enormous, and then searing, terrible pain.

Then nothing.

Quietly, Rance let the body slide to the ground. He wiped his blade on his britches and smiled. There was nothing like a nice, clean, knife kill.

And that was a extra good one, wasn't it? The town sheriff. Imagine a fellow like that having the balls to ride down the middle of the street in a town Rance Carthage had staked out for his own. Rance guessed that the skinny sheriff had more gumption than he had given him credit for.

And, he was happy to note, he'd learned that his primary target were all on the same building, all up on the bank's roof.

Sitting ducks, all in a row. Blam, blam, blam.

And hadn't it been real thoughtful of them to tuck all the women and kids in one place? Why, he believed he'd give Slocum a real big thank-you.

Right before he killed him.

25

"Did you hear somethin'?" Slocum asked. There had been a sound, down in the alley.

"Just the sheriff, goin' in the bank," whispered Blue in reply. His glasses, hanging by one earpiece, dangled precariously from his breast pocket.

"Best get those or you'll lose 'em," Slocum said softly, pointing.

"Thanks," Blue said, and tucked them back in. "He's sure takin' his time, ain't he?"

Boots scratched the adobe clay of the roof, and Amos crawled over. "I'm beginning to wonder if we haven't already killed him," he whispered. And then he added, more brightly, "I say, that'd certainly take the cake, wouldn't it, if he were lying out there dead someplace on the desert? And here we are, all primed and ready, with the citizenry armed to the teeth and scared half to death." He paused. "And the women ready to beat us to death."

"At least one woman," Slocum replied with a grunt. "Bet she could do it, too."

"Who?" asked Blue.

"A rather imposing-looking woman downstairs,"

Amos said, "who informed Slocum and myself that the townspeople had taken care of this Rance Carthage once already with eggs and cabbages and such. She indicated that they could do it again, if necessary."

Blue snorted. "Hope you set her right."

Slocum was no longer thinking about the testy woman downstairs, though. If he was thinking about any woman it was little Honey, from last night. She was down there, too. He sure hoped they lived so that he could buy her something nice.

Maybe shoes. Gals liked shoes.

He cleared his throat—and cleared thoughts of Honey from his head—and said, "All right. Back to your posts, boys."

Amos shook his head. "And here I thought I was in charge."

Blue slapped him on the back. "You just keep on thinkin' that way, Amos," he said with a grin before he scuttled back into position.

Amos rolled his eyes. "I am surrounded by men who believe they are comedians." Then, without waiting for a reply from Slocum, he crept back to his place, across the roof.

Slocum turned to stare out across the desert once more.

And he thought, *Come on, Rance, you crazy bastard. Come on if you're comin'.*

•   •   •

Rance was nearly directly below Slocum, hugging the wall, his breath coming shallow. The thrill of the hunt was on him, so much that when he'd thought about going on into the bank and taking the women hostage, he'd brushed the idea aside.

Logically, he knew it was probably his best chance of owning the town.

He knew he could get himself all the ass he wanted while he was waiting.

He also knew he wouldn't hurt for food or water, no matter how long he had to hole up in there. After all, the menfolk wouldn't let the women suffer any, now would they?

But the blood lust, the chance to take out Slocum and the Englishman, was too strong. He wanted them dead, dead for himself and for his brothers, and he wanted to get started on it right now.

Not that he wanted it to end all that soon, of course. He wanted them to linger. A long time.

When the whispers from up on the roof settled down and he heard men scrambling back into position, he let himself relax a little.

Now, he'd been all the way around the bank, and the only outside staircase he'd found had looked like a skinny rat would get it to squeak.

He was no skinny rat, he knew.

So he decided to do the next best thing. He'd go to the roof next door. It was easy enough. He'd already done it on three different rooftops, and either stabbed to death or throttled five lookouts, male and female alike.

So, quietly, he made his way around the next building, making sure to go clear around to its far side so that Slocum and his buddies wouldn't see him going up the stairs.

He started up.

Three steps up, a step complained.

He stopped.

"Who goes there?" came the hissed challenge from the rooftop.

"It's me, you fool," Rance hissed. "Frank." Frank somebody-or-other had been his first kill of the night, and was the only townsman's name that he knew, on account of that kid calling out.

It had worked so far, anyhow.

"Come on up," the rooftop voice whispered. "What you doin' out of position? I thought you was down by the Feed and Grain!"

"Was," Rance said softly, just before his head bobbed up into the lookout's line of sight. "Ain't no more," he added, and threw his knife.

The blade took the man—a kind of tall, skinny, rangy fellow—right dead center in the chest, killing him instantly. He fell with too loud a thud, and Rance scrambled up, over the edge, and lay down as flat and as fast as he could.

"Marcus!" a voice called, the tone low but unmistakable. The Englishman! "Marcus Webber, are you all right?"

"Slipped and fell," hissed Rance, just loud enough to be heard on the next building. He hugged that roof like nobody's business.

"Show me," said the Englishman.

Rance scowled, had a few particularly nasty thoughts about what he'd be showing that limey in a few minutes, then held up his rifle.

That would be the only part of him that they'd be able to see, he hoped. His arm and his rifle.

Amos frowned and wrinkled his forehead.

"Slocum," he whispered softly, "does that look like Marcus Webber's arm to you?"

Slocum crawled over. "Who's Marcus Webber?"

Amos tipped his head. "Next roof over."

Slocum looked, his brow furrowing. "Ain't he a tall, skinny feller?"

Amos nodded.

Slocum set down his rifle and quietly drew his handgun. "If it is, he'd been doin' a whole lot of blacksmithin' since he went up top that roof."

"My thoughts exactly," Amos concurred.

Blue looked over and started to come their way, but Amos held out his hand, then held a finger to his lips. He pointed to the next building over.

Blue, suddenly serious, nodded.

Blue and Slocum were looking terribly solemn all

of a sudden. Amos supposed that he was, too, and asked, "How do you feel we should handle this?"

"Real goddamn careful," said Slocum, and checked his sidearm again. "I'll go down. Hope I can do it quiet, but if I can't, cover me. But stay down flat. That damned Rance can shoot the eyes out of a horsefly on the wing."

He started to move away, but Amos caught his arm. "And why the bloody hell do you get to go over there?" he demanded softly.

This was his job, after all, whether he'd brought Slocum along or not. Blue, too, for that matter. It was his place to go over and face Rance Carthage.

"Because I drew straws when you wasn't lookin'," and I lost," Slocum said, annoyed. "Sides, you only got one good arm."

There were some things about John Slocum that Amos would never be able to understand. For instance, why, when danger was imminent, Slocum was always the first one to plunge into it. Perhaps he felt that he was the only one who could save himself. Amos didn't know.

But he said, "Hold on, Slocum. We need a better plan."

"You got one?"

"Not exactly," said Amos, lifting his brows. "But I'm thinking."

Both their heads turned at a quiet little *plop* and *crackle* sound off the far edge of the bank's roof.

And they both noticed, at the same moment, that Blue was gone.

"Shit," Slocum swore under his breath, then turned back toward Amos. Quickly, he whispered, "I'm goin' now. I'm gonna try to catch Blue. He goes up from one side, I go up from the other." He paused. "That building's got two ways up, don't it?"

Amos nodded yes.

"You stay here, and when I signal you, stand up," Slocum said, all in a breathless rush. "That's the only way you can see down into that roof, since it's the same height as this one. If it's really Rance over there, just start shootin' at him."

He started toward the far side of the roof, thinking that he was going to have to jump down.

Great.

Damn that Blue, anyhow, showing off! Skipping the stairs and aping Blue was the only way he could get down to the ground without making a squeak or a creak.

As an afterthought, he turned his head back toward Amos. "And try not to shoot me or Blue," he added.

Faintly, he heard Amos mutter something or other, but paid it no mind. Dragging himself to the edge of the roof, he checked down below. There was Blue, grinning up at him and dusting off his britches.

"Damn your hide!" Slocum mouthed.

He holstered his gun and eased himself off the side until he was hanging by his hands. He felt Blue's hand on his boot, steadying him. He let go.

Miraculously, he landed on his feet, although Blue being there to direct his fall helped some. He didn't mention it, however. Briefly, almost silently, he brought Blue up to speed on the plan.

"Rance already got Sheriff Coltrane," Blue said, after Slocum was done. "Over there." He tipped his head, indicating a dark shape on the ground, near the wall. "The bastard gutted him like a fish."

Slocum drew his gun again. "That sonofabitch can't be dead soon enough, far as I'm concerned."

He had never meant anything so much in his life.

Blue simply and grimly, nodded in agreement.

Quietly, guns drawn, they started making their way around the back of the bank.

Slocum turned in at the near side of the building, crept to the foot of the stair, and waited for Blue to make his way around the other side.

Always, his head was turned upward, watching, watching for any sign of movement.

And he knew those old wooden steps were going to squeal when they went up, so he'd told Blue to just startle the hell out of Rance and take them at a run. The same way he planned to.

If they panicked the bastard enough, maybe he'd only get one of them before they got him.

Or maybe he'd stand up—or at least sit up—and Amos could take him out.

Any which way you looked at it, it was a tricky situation, and one with which the townspeople couldn't possibly help.

In fact, they'd be a hindrance.

Oh, he'd thought about just yelling out that Rance Carthage was up on top of the mercantile. But what good would that do?

If folks just started shooting from their present positions, the town would likely kill half its own population in the crossfire.

And if they came down, Rance would have them at his mercy. Lord knows how much ammo he'd hauled up there with him.

If Slocum was any judge, Rance wasn't the kind of man to go around under-armed.

So it had come to this.

Slocum knew that Rance could, and likely would, take at least one of them out before they got him. Blue knew it, too. So did Amos.

He felt pretty damned rotten about that part, about Blue, that was. He and Amos had signed up for this years ago, the first time they'd gone out after the Carthage boys, but Blue was more or less an innocent bystander. There was nothing he could do about it, though. Now, it was up to God or the fates. They'd all do the best they could.

Including, he supposed, Rance Carthage.

He heard a *chuck-chuck, chuck-chuck* sound from the opposite side of the building.

Blue was in place, and signaling that he was ready.

Slocum took a deep breath, then bolted up the stairs two at a time, hollering like a banshee rebel.

26

Blue was screaming, too, but when they gained the rooftop there was no one there, and they were hollering at each other.

Well, no one except the body of the late Marcus Webber, knifed through the heart.

Slocum barely had time to take this in when he heard a shot from behind him.

As one, he and Blue turned toward the sound, dropping to the rooftop as they did, and Slocum just saw Amos's hat as he fell. Or dropped down. He couldn't tell.

But then a voice carried over the rooftops. Rance Carthage called, "Got your little English buddy, Slocum. You're next."

Slocum shouted, "In your dreams!" and rolled.

As he expected, Rance fired toward the sound, and a slug dug into the adobe where Slocum had been when he shouted.

Amos. Amos, dead?

But he couldn't stop to think about that now. He and Blue had a whole town counting on them.

"Get you, Slocum?" Rance shouted, and then he laughed.

"Pert near," Slocum replied, signaling Blue as he rolled again. From the corner of his eye, he saw Blue slip over the side of the building as Rance's second slug put a new hole in the mercantile roof.

Slocum figured he was going to run out of places to roll before long. Blue had better hurry.

"Goddamn it, Rance!" he shouted, hoping to keep him distracted.

He rolled again, this time in a different direction. It was a good thing he'd changed course, because this time Rance's bullet struck in the place where Slocum would have been, if he'd kept moving the way he had been.

Where was Blue?

He gritted his teeth and shouted again. "Nice try, you sonofabitch!"

Again, he rolled, and Rance fired. "If nothin' else, Slocum, I'm makin' you get your exercise!" he shouted, then cackled as if he'd made a wildly inventive joke.

Slocum was close enough that with the next roll, he could get behind the building's low chimney. It wasn't much protection, but it was some.

He shouted, "And you're gonna die tonight, Rance!"

He practically threw his body back behind the

short, slender, adobe chimney just as Rance's slug glanced off it, right at roof level.

Slocum heaved a little sigh of relief.

Holding his body sideways, he rose up behind the slim chimney a little way, took off his hat, and peered around the stack with one eye.

The roof across the way showed no movement. Rance was down, biding his time.

But his voice rose up. "Are you dead, yet, Slocum? Hope not. Just like to wound you a little, that's all."

"Why's that?" Slocum shouted back, hoping against hope that he'd lift his head.

But he didn't, not this time. Instead, he shouted, "Got plans for you, Slocum. Gonna haul you down into the street. Gonna make you take a real long time to die. Gonna string your guts out, Comanche style, and let you watch the dogs eat 'em."

Somebody, back behind Slocum on another roof, lost his lunch rather loudly, and once again, Rance Carthage laughed.

And then, Slocum saw the very top of Blue's head peek over the far rim of the bank's roof. He tensed. "Sounds real entertainin' Rance!" he called, hoping to distract him long enough for Blue to get off a shot.

He wished he hadn't put the women and kids in the bank. He wished he had some more of that dynamite. He'd signal Blue to drop from the roof, then blow Rance Carthage to hell, where he belonged.

All this, he wished in the split second that it took for Blue to pop up, fire, then drop back down.

Rance let out a yelp, then Slocum heard him scrambling. He fired at the sound.

"Missed me, you bastard," Rance called.

"Somebody hit you," Slocum shouted back.

And Rance finally popped up to take another shot at Slocum.

Slocum fired.

He saw the shot knock Rance back a few feet, and then he dropped out of sight.

From somewhere out of sight, he heard Blue call, "You get him?"

Slocum's eyes were narrowed. "Wouldn't count on it if I was you."

Now Rance was wounded, but there was nothing more dangerous than a wounded animal. And Slocum reminded himself that they thought they'd put an end to him once before. The man was damned near impossible to kill.

Slocum was just preparing to stand up, take his chances and fire another slug into Rance, when Blue popped up again.

He fired, but the fire was returned quickly, and with a tiny cry, Blue fell. Slocum heard him crash down the steps, then nothing.

"Sure hope he ain't dead, Slocum," Rance called.

The bastard didn't even sound hurt! "I'd like to stake him out next to you."

Blue and Amos, both dead. Killed by this goddamn pig of a man. *No, that was an insult to pigs.*

But in the space of less than five minutes, Carthage had killed two of the best friends Slocum had ever known. It wounded him deeply, but he didn't have time to feel it. He couldn't let himself. Neither could he allow himself to feel the rage boiling in his veins.

He ground his teeth for a moment, gathering himself, then shouted, "Rufus didn't die right away, you know. He was all blown to pieces, but he hung on for a good hour. Must take after you, Rance."

Silence.

And then, Rance said, "He couldn't have. You blowed that place apart."

"He was in terrible pain, Rance," Slocum continued. He kept his gun aimed at the opposite roof. No shooting at sounds, this time. He wanted a clean head shot.

"Blew off both arms and a leg," he went on, trying to add as much joy to his voice as possible. "Blew the skin right off his face. Nose and an ear was gone, too. But we fixed him up so that he lived for a while." Slocum paused. "Did, too. Course, he was screamin' most of the time."

"Liar!"

"Believe me or not," Slocum shouted. "No skin off my back."

With an outraged shout of "You sonofabitch!" Rance stood up all the way and started shooting at the chimney—and Slocum. There was no time for Slocum to get a shot off. All he could do was hit the deck.

But somebody *did* get a shot off, because quite suddenly, Rance stopped firing. Slocum peeked around the chimney and saw him, surprised and wavering.

Slocum brought up his gun and aimed right for the center of Rance's forehead.

He didn't miss.

Rance went down—this time, hopefully for good—and Slocum, who had just discovered that one of Rance's slugs had nicked him in the calf, limped quickly down the stairs.

"Is he dead?" asked a tremulous male voice, high up somewhere above him.

"Wait," was all Slocum said. He'd sure like to know who fired that shot. He hoped it had been Blue, but he knew better than to try to fool himself into believing he was still alive.

He rounded the side of the bank, saw Blue's body there at the foot of the steps, took a deep breath and stepped over it. Gun drawn, he started up the creaky steps.

He peered over the rim of the roof, and finally

relaxed. Rance lay sprawled, his gun fallen from his outstretched hand. Blood trickled from a neat hole in the center of his forehead.

But Slocum didn't holster his gun. He still didn't trust the nine-lived sonofabitch.

He stepped over the rim and made his way toward the body. He kicked it. It didn't move. He kicked it more savagely. Still nothing.

But he aimed his pistol downward, and in rapid succession, fired three more slugs straight down into Rance Carthage's brain.

The body jumped with each impact, then lay still again. The face was now unrecognizable.

And Slocum? He felt damn good about it. Damned satisfied. Still, there was something missing.

There was silence, as if the town itself was holding its breath.

And then, a soft whisper. "Oh, shoot him just once more, for me."

Slocum's head jerked up, and he broke out in a grin. "Amos?"

Two days later, Slocum was back in Hoopskirt, in Lucy's soft bed, smoking a cigar and trying to explain the last few days' events.

"Tell me about Blue," Lucy asked. She was naked and beautiful, a thin sheen of sweat covering her from head to toe, and she lay beside him, curled under his arm.

There hadn't been a chance for questions when he first walked in the saloon. He had just wanted her, and wanted her now.

"He'll be fine, thank God," Slocum said, staring up at the ceiling. Ceilings made him think of rooftops, and rooftops made him think of Rance, and that was highly unpleasant. He looked over at Lucy, instead.

Better.

"I thought he was dead at first. But when I came down the stairs haulin' Amos, he moved. Just a little bit," he said. "Be a few weeks before he's on his feet again. Your doc's takin' good care of him."

"And the Carthage brothers?" she asked. "That Rance, especially!"

"Boys got blown up," he said, taking a puff on his cigar. He blew out the smoke in a soft plume. "And as for Rance . . . well, I told you that we killed him. And then the townsfolk, once they got hold of his body. . . ."

"What?" she urged.

"They tore him apart. With their bare hands."

Slocum had never seen anything like it, and he never hoped to again. He didn't know that decent people could be like that. But then, he wasn't so certain that the people of Crowfoot were all that decent.

To his surprise, Lucy said, "Good. He deserved it."

He gave his head an almost imperceptible shake. "Bloodthirsty little bitch, ain't you?"

She sighed, then gave a little shudder. "Guess so. I hope there ain't many more out there like 'em. And if there are, I sure hope they don't cross my path. I've lost enough friends to last a lifetime, thanks."

Dutch and Harry, too, Slocum thought. He and Amos had found Dutch's bay when they were carting Blue home in the wagon. The Lord only knew what had happened to Harry's sorrel.

And Blue was hurt pretty bad. Rance's shot had taken him in the side, grazing a lung, but it had been the fall that had done him the worst. He had two broken legs, an arm, a collarbone, and suffered a concussion. He'd be laid up for a good, long time.

"And your English friend, Amos?" Lucy asked. "He looks just fine to me. I mean, considering."

"If you mean considering that he got clipped in the side here in town, then in the shoulder the night we blew up the first two Carthages, and then shot in the neck that last night? Yeah, I'd say he was doing pretty goddamned good." Slocum smiled and shook his head. "He's one lucky sonofabitch."

Actually, Amos had lost quite a bit of blood, but had the presence of mind to press a bandanna over his neck wound with one hand while he was trying to grope for his gun—without Rance seeing—with the other.

The local doc had patched him up, and he was currently across the hall with one of the other girls. Doubtless, bragging about his exploit and coaxing out all the sympathy he could get.

"I'd say you fellers did yourselves proud out there," Lucy said, and ran her hand down his chest, down his belly, and took his already swelling cock into her little hand.

"Don't know about proud," he said, remembering the way he'd felt when he pumped those extra shots into Rance Carthage's face. "But we got the job done, anyhow."

He didn't add that he'd finally gotten a straight answer out of Amos about the pay. It was five hundred, and it was being wired to him today, along, Amos said, with the thanks of a grateful nation.

He didn't much care about the grateful nation part. His leg had stopped bothering him—it had only been nicked, after all—and right now he was feeling as randy as hell.

He dropped his cigar in the ashtray, turned toward Lucy, and smiling, he kissed her.

DON'T MISS A YEAR OF

SLOCUM GIANT

BY

JAKE LOGAN

SLOCUM GIANT 2001:

SLOCUM AND THE HELPLESS HARLETS

0-515-13136-9

SLOCUM GIANT 2002:

SLOCUM AND THE CARNAHAN BOYS

0-515-13384-1

SLOCUM GIANT 2003:

THE GUNMAN AND THE GREENHORN

0-515-13639-5

**AVAILABLE WHEREVER BOOKS ARE SOLD OR AT
WWW.PENGUIN.COM**

B900

JAKE LOGAN
TODAY'S HOTTEST ACTION WESTERN!

AVAILABLE WHEREVER BOOKS ARE SOLD OR AT
WWW.PENGUIN.COM

(Ad # B110)

LONGARM

Explore the exciting Old West with one of the men who made it wild!

AVAILABLE WHEREVER BOOKS ARE SOLD OR AT
WWW.PENGUIN.COM

J. R. ROBERTS

THE GUNSMITH